DEATH IN A TENURED POSITION
AMANDA CROSS
A Kate Fansler Mystery

Also by Amanda Cross
Published by Ballantine Books:

THE JAMES JOYCE MURDER

DEATH IN A
Tenured Position

Amanda Cross

BALLANTINE BOOKS • NEW YORK

Grateful acknowledgment is made for permission to reprint "Myth." Copyright 1978, by McGraw Hill. Reprinted from The Collected Poems of Muriel Rukeyser, by permission of International Creative Management.

Library of Congress Catalog Card Number: 80-20565

ISBN 0-345-32950-3

This edition published by arrangement with E.P. Dutton

Manufactured in the United States of America

First Ballantine Books Edition: May 1982
Seventh Printing: June 1985

To May Sarton

Since Harvard University, Cambridge, many of the places and some of the people mentioned in this novel do exist, it is the more important to declare unequivocally that none of the persons actually appearing in this novel, connected or unconnected with Harvard, bears any resemblance to anyone anywhere. To emphasize the truth of this assertion particularly in regard to Harvard's English Department, the author states that she has met a very few tenured members of that department, and is acquainted with only one, who does not appear in this story. The author has entered Warren House only once, uninvited, to case the joint for the purpose of writing this book.

Prologue

If there are among you, as I hope there are, any impatient friends of women's education, as Joseph Warner called them, I can think of no better way to serve the cause than to establish a number of Radcliffe chairs at Harvard. The field of the professorship doesn't matter, so long as it is held by a woman.
GILES CONSTABLE
Radcliffe Centennial News

ANDREW SLADOVSKI, Assistant Professor of English, Harvard University, to Peter Sarkins, Assistant Professor of English, Washington University, St. Louis:

Dear Peter: You will have been trying to guess, even before you opened the envelope, what could have inspired old Andy to write. Stop guessing, you never will. Harvard is about to have a woman professor in the English Department! We are all buzzing like Tennyson's innumerable bees, or was it Poe's? Needless to say, Hopkins, our ever-lovable chairman, is fit to be tied. He had just announced to the assembled English faculty that he thought the woman problem had peaked and we needn't worry about hiring one anymore, when this came upon him. If the guy weren't such a shit, I could find it in my heart to pity him. Of course, they are all worried about menopause—it is absolutely all they can think of when a woman threatens to penetrate their masculine precincts—how revealing language is. No one knows who it will be, but I am hoping for a very feminist type who will give them what for. Bloody unlikely. Lizzy says they will manage to find a well-

1

known scholar who thinks any woman could have made it, since she did. She wants, incidentally, to add a snide note to this letter. . . .

Allen Adam Clarkville, Professor of English, Harvard University, to Mark Peterson Mattias, Professor of English in the same university, on leave:

Dear Peterson: One wonders if the news can possibly have escaped you at Bellagio. My guess, since no fearsome telegrams have arrived, is that you are off in the mountains and have not heard. Do not, Peterson, lose yourself on an Alp, I need all the support life can offer. Some beastly millionaire has offered Harvard a million dollars for a professorship in the English Department, provided the holder is a woman. No doubt the happy fact that we have never had a woman professor made us a delicious target for this beneficence. And no palming her off on History and Lit. Talk about fluttering the dovecotes. I really do think these hetero types are more terrified of women than we are. And Hopkins had actually thought we might continue the separation of the sexes after dinner at parties. I shall not quote Sam Johnson on preaching women, but will leave that to old Fronsy. If it didn't mean that I should have to sit staring at her in meetings for the rest of my professional life, I would almost exalt at the frenzy hereabouts. Apparently Harvard will not turn down a million dollars, however hysterical our yelps. What's more, whoever he is (has anyone ever studied the phenomenon of the male feminist, John Stuart Mill leaps, of course, immediately to mind?) is rumored to have promised another million for a second female professor if this one works out. One scarcely knows whether to cheer or sabotage. I need hardly tell you what I suspect of going through the minds of some of our stately colleagues. . . .

Frank Williams, Professor of English, Harvard University, to Frederick Held, Professor of English, Columbia University:

Dear Fred: You will guess why I am writing. Con-

sider this a formal request for a suggestion for someone: female, scholarly, to fill the by now much publi-
cized chair. The president quite rightly refuses to refuse
the money, though some pressure has been brought
upon him. You shall have my views viva voce before
long. Since I am, for my sins, head of the search committee, I must come up with someone, and you have
more women around there, and know more at other
universities than do the rest of us—due of course to
your rightly celebrated sweet and unprejudiced nature.
The dame we seek ought to be well established and, if
possible, not given to hysterical scenes. We are firmly
told that stalling will not be allowed, but in exchange
for an agreed-upon deadline, I am allowed to have no
women on the search committee. Howls will go up from
the Radcliffe quarter—they have, of course, been
promised a say in *everything* to do with women (if only
women had stayed happily confined within those female
ranks)—but I hold firm. This department *will* make
one final all-male decision.

The bodies that must be spinning in their graves. I
intend to be cremated myself. Hopkins, I need hardly tell
you, is beside himself—an ancient and accurate description. Fran has lifted the perfect phrase for the occasion from a recent Iris Murdoch novel: *Sic biscuitus
disintegrat:* that's how the cookie crumbles. A wonderful thought occurs to me. Do you think we could get
Iris Murdoch? We would take her respected husband,
John Bayley, too, a *fine* critic; he could teach the
course (husbands must have some rights left) and she
could quietly write her novels. That's the pleasantest
thought I've had since this dreary business began. . . .

Chapter 1

Disillusionment in living is the finding out nobody agrees with you. . . . The amount they agree is important to you until the amount they do not agree with you is completely realized by you. Then you say you will write for yourself and strangers, you will be for yourself and strangers and this then makes an old man or an old woman of you.
GERTRUDE STEIN
Making of Americans

KATE FANSLER gazed across the large conference table at the men on its other side, and the men on either side of her. The other woman member of the committee was black, female and absent today. She had so many demands on her time and attention that occasionally her committee assignments overlapped, even when the committee was as prestigious as this one. Kate decided, gazing around at the male faces, long trained to hide irritation but not boredom, that this decade would be marked for her by the sitting around tables, large, highly polished, conference tables, in the company of many men, and a few women, whose assignment was to grapple with the problems of academia in the seventies. Kate would sometimes picture her tombstone with "The Token Woman" engraved in the marble. Above the inscription, androgynous angels would indifferently float.

At five she rose to her feet, determined to lie her way out of the room. One of the men, she knew, would leave soon to catch his car pool, and she would precede him by only minutes. The fact was, she was tired to death of male pomposities and long-windedness and had, in any case, to move about or scream. No one, of course, much noticed her departure, though there were a few perfunctory waves. She hoped that whatever marked the eighties, it would not be committee meetings. Something if not more exciting, at least less—well, token.

Once out of the room, Kate somewhat revived. She would go home, have a drink and put her feet up. Reed, junketing about the world to advise on police methods, might have written. To be more accurate, the post office might have been inspired to deliver his letter. Stopping for a moment in the women's room on the ground floor, Kate gazed amused at a small circular plaque pasted to the mirror: "Trust in God: She will provide." Kate smiled and set out for home.

There were those, Kate thought, sipping her martini and letting the day settle down in her mind, who would have said that God, of whatever sex or authenticity, had provided Kate with quite enough. No argument there. Born to wealth and position, Kate had had the rare benefits of her family's advantages while evading what she considered their overwhelming drawbacks. Which, freely translated, meant the privilege of wealth, but not the opinions or conventions. Determined to be a professional woman when such a determination was, in her milieu, more than mildly eccentric, she had become a Professor of Literature at one of New York's largest and most prestigious universities. Late in life—at least as these things go—she had married a man who offered companionship rather than dizzy rapture; they had neither of them chosen to view marriage as an unending alternation between lust and dinner in the best restaurants. Reed Amhearst had entered her life as an Assistant District Attorney; he still operated in the higher reaches of the police world, though in recent years his efforts had veered sharply toward the preservation of humaneness in law enforcement. His present sojourn in Africa was in a cause dear to his heart. At this hour, even after his absence of weeks, Kate listened for his footsteps.

Kate's languors, as she realized, were the price of an accomplished life. Or, to put it in a more high-flown way appropriate to Kate's profession, one sank into the ancient sin of anomie when challenges failed. Odd, Kate thought, the years it took to learn one simple fact: that the prize just ahead, the next job, publication, love affair, marriage always seemed to hold the key to satisfaction but never, in the longer run, sufficed. However one tried to savor one's gifts—leisure, health, money, a room of one's own—one always ended peering ahead, to the next chance. This had been marked for Kate, in her childhood, by her mother's friends who seemed constantly to move and to redecorate houses and apartments. And now, such was life today, even if one survived the worst, one reached a condition sharply modern, at least described with a modern phrase: survivor guilt. And so one asked: What next, what new purpose to life, what new community or service?

Kate, mixing herself another martini and putting off thoughts of dinner, admitted that she had, perhaps through some such sense of darkness where, as Ecclesiastes says, desire fails, been lured into the solving of crimes. With Reed's help, of course. Did everyone have friends and acquaintances who found themselves caught in such dramas of death and passion? Doris Lessing had recently written that the bonds of realism in the novel are loosening, because "what we see around us becomes daily wilder, more fantastic, incredible." Kate believed her.

She had, however, been long unemployed as a detective. One did not wish for bodies, heaven knew; the world could ill afford another single gesture of violence. For what then did she wish? The sense, perhaps, that she had not passed the point where she might affect events; move the world, however slightly, in the direction of humaneness. She and Reed, then, halfway around the world from one another, were after the same thing. But he was engaged; she sat at round tables among pompous men, beginning, for the first time in a life devoted to language and ideas, to question the efficacy of both.

Kate, calling up purpose enough at least for this, carried her glass into the kitchen and contemplated dinner. Not the sin of anomie, she decided, whipping eggs with a fork; it was rather what the French call *aboulie: l'absence morbide de volonté*. What nonsense, Kate said, reaching for the omelet pan. If you are not careful, she admonished herself, you will begin to sound like one of George Eliot's purposeless heroines on whom you lecture so unceasingly. I at least, Kate thought, am instructed to trust in God, waiting for Her to provide.

The woman was leaning against Kate's office door when Kate arrived the next afternoon for her office hours. Sitting near her, its haunches drawn beneath it in an agony of restlessness, was a large white bullterrier, the sort of beast who looked like a child's drawing of a dog. Vaguely, Kate recalled a sign on the outermost door of Baldwin Hall: *No Dogs Allowed*.

"You're Kate," the woman said. It was unclear if this was a question or an answer. Kate, searching for her key, nodded. The dog rose, with what might have been menace, to its feet. "Down, you bitch," the woman said in even tones. "Might I see you a minute? Are you afraid of dogs? I can leave Jocasta outside."

"Come in," Kate said, "and bring, er, Jocasta with you." They all entered the room, Jocasta, in Kate's opinion, looking insufficiently grateful for the invitation.

"Thanks," the woman said. She removed her down jacket, revealing a T-shirt with a picture of Virginia Woolf on it, and workmanlike trousers. Her long, straight hair hung down on both sides of her face; she wore large spectacles. Her movements were those of a female body which has eschewed all small motions; late thirties, Kate thought, or maybe forties, what the hell difference does it make?

"Please sit down."

"My name is Joan Theresa," the woman said, dropping into the chair near Kate's desk. "Down, Jocasta, lie down and stay down." Jocasta, again resting uneasily on her haunches, allowed her front legs to slide forward so that she was, within the meaning of the act, lying down. Every muscle denied that she was relaxed; her gaze rested upon Kate.

"You don't know me," Joan Theresa said. "I live in Cambridge. Mass, that is; some of us run a coffee shop called Maybe Next Time. On Hampshire Street. Jocasta, you bitch, lie down and stay down or you'll go back on canned dog food. Sorry"—turning to Kate— "I'm afraid you make her nervous. Not you, of course, this place. You wonder why I'm here."

Wonder, Kate thought, yes, I wonder, but not too much. What is there to wonder about these days? "Were you thinking of moving to New York?" Kate asked. "Attending this university?"

"This shit house! Sorry. You took me by surprise. No, I just came down to see you. A favor to someone."

"Would it bother you," Kate asked, "if I smoked?"

"Yes, it would," Joan Theresa said. "It makes me sick."

Kate returned her cigarette to the pack. "How can I help you?" she asked, she hoped not impatiently, "except by not smoking, and not making Jocasta nervous."

"I don't mean to be rude. They told me you were straight, but not how straight. Your name is Kate Fansler. Is Fansler your husband's name?"

"No. It's my father's name. Theresa, I take it, is your mother's."

"Now that's clever," Joan Theresa said. "I like your saying that." Something in her body and, Kate noticed, Jocasta's, relaxed. Nothing obvious, but the tenseness was gone. Jocasta let her head touch the floor. Still, Kate was aware of being scrutinized. The raincoat Kate had hung up was a fashionable raincoat. Her shoes, though flat, were fashionable shoes. Her panty hose covered shaved legs. Her suit, ultra-suede, was worn

over a turtleneck knit, and on her jacket was a pin: a
gold pin. Kate was dressed for the patriarchy.

"My clothes," Kate said, "make my life easier, as
yours make your life easier. Is there something you want
from me?"

"Not for me," Joan said. "For Janet Mandelbaum.
She said you would remember her. Mandelbaum is her
husband's name, but they're divorced."

"I know," Kate said.

"I had a husband once," Joan said. She shifted in her
chair, and the dog rose hesitantly to a sitting position.

"Down, girl. Do you know what finally broke up my
marriage? This was in my trying to be the good wife
phase. Before I took my mother's first name for my
last. My husband, who had been having a rough time
generally trying to make out in the world, found horse
manure in the bedroom. He really thought I'd gone to
the trouble to shovel it up, or maybe bring a horse in,
just so he could step into horse manure in his bedroom.
The truth, for which he never listened, was much simpler and without malice. Jocasta here was young then,
and used to eat everything with an interesting smell. I
was walking her in the park, and she ate some horse
manure. By the time we had returned home, and I'd
fallen into bed in compliance with my husband's lust,
Jocasta had decided that the horse manure wasn't sitting right, and she upchucked it, quite unchanged, onto
the bedroom floor. I like to think that Jocasta was up-
chucking her horse manure at the same moment my
husband was . . . well, never mind. There is a moral
to the story, which is connected with why I am here.
Men will always suppose you have put the horse manure there on purpose to spite them."

Silence fell, while Kate thought about Janet Mandelbaum, who had, it seemed, inspired this extraordinary
visit. Kate had recently read that Janet had gone to
Harvard as the first woman professor in the English
Department. Janet, of course, was not Jewish; Mandelbaum had represented Janet's main and only liberal
phase. She had kept the name because it was with that

name that she had made her reputation: an impressive reputation. Hers had certainly been the most important study of seventeenth-century poetry since T. S. Eliot's, and back in the 1950s seventeenth-century poetry had been where the action was. Nothing could change the scholarly reputation that book had produced. It had led, several less impressive books later, to Harvard. The less impressive books had, however, been solid, reputable, safe.

"Janet was never a feminist," Kate said.

"I wouldn't say that." Joan reinforced the sarcasm with her gestures. "She was never a *woman,* professionally speaking."

"I know," Kate said. "I assumed that was why Harvard had taken her. She had also had a hysterectomy, when young, and could therefore be guaranteed not to have a menopause, during which all women go mad, as everyone knows. To be frank, I can't imagine you and Janet acquainted. A most unlikely combination, in fact."

"Most. The fact is, Janet's in trouble. And the sisters are involved."

"The sisters?"

"A commune. Not religious, just a group of women who support each other."

"On Hampshire Street."

"You learn fast. It takes brains to make it in the system, I recognize that. Janet was found in an inebriated state in an ancient bathroom in some old frame house where the English Department hangs out, and the sisters are implicated. We had nothing to do with it."

At that point there came a knock on the door. Kate rose to open it. Outside stood a graduate student, male. His eyes rested upon Jocasta, who returned his gaze with a growl, rising ominously. Kate stepped outside, shutting the door behind her. "Mr. Marshall," she said, "I know you had an appointment. Would you mind giving me a few minutes? Wait down the hall until you see my, er, guests leave. All right?" Mr. Marshall nodded, never taking his eyes from Kate. The story will be all over the department in ten minutes, Kate thought. But what story?

The three of them met, that evening, in Kate's apartment. Kate lounged with her feet up, Joan Theresa sat cross-legged on the floor, and Jocasta slept on the couch. Kate was drinking Scotch, Joan was drinking coffee and Kate was smoking. A fan had been set to blow the smoke away from Joan Theresa.

"Don't tell me I ought to give it up," Kate said. "I know. I have tried, often. I hate the fact that I smoke, and hate myself even worse when I don't. What on earth is happening with Janet at Harvard?"

Jocasta turned on the couch with a contented grunt; Joan shifted her legs. "Finding Janet Mandelbaum and one of the sisters in anything together is as likely as finding Nixon campaigning for Ted Kennedy. No way, no way at all. But, there they are. I gathered before you didn't know what a sister is, not really."

"Not really, I guess. You don't mean, obviously, that all women are sisters, as the French speak of fraternity."

"I doubt very much that all men are brothers, or ever have been, though they bond tightly enough with their own kind, but women who are sisters have no part in the male establishment, no part in patriarchal institutions at all. Furthermore, they despise them. They feel that patriarchal institutions have suppressed and used women, and the sisters want nothing to do with them; they would, in fact, like to destroy them, but at least they know they're rotten. Women who are not sisters play along with the rottenness, either liking it, or thinking it changeable."

"Like me."

"Forgive me, yes."

"And the desire of sisters is to blow up these institutions, literally if possible."

"No, not literally. Violence and destruction and injury are male games. But they will use the male institutions for their own purposes, if they can. They will lie;

they do not trust, because that trust has always been betrayed. To a woman like me, Janet Mandelbaum is worse than a man, she conspires with men against other women. We have no use for women who live with men, in their work or anywhere."

"I, of course," Kate said, "wish to reserve the right to be seen as different from Janet Mandelbaum. There are degrees."

"Would you have gone to Harvard, if asked? Or Yale? Or Princeton, it makes no difference?"

"As a matter of fact I wouldn't have, but not for the honorable reasons that implies. First, I would find myself on every committee, overused, and underattended too. Second, I find Harvard, where the Fansler men have gone for generations, hideously complacent, like themselves, and unlikely to grow less so. Henry James wrote a novel in the 1890s in which a young woman shows an admirer around Harvard, pointing out each of the buildings and remarking that there is no place for women in them; Harvard hasn't changed much since. Little more than ten years ago, women could not use many of the libraries. No, for whatever reasons, I would not have gone if asked, nor to Yale or Princeton either. That, however, makes me no different from Janet, or not enough different to count."

"Yes."

"Why, then, are you here? Why is Jocasta so beautifully snoring on my couch? Am I so suspect that you scorn women who work with the patriarchy, but are not above turning to them in need?"

"You certainly lay it on the line."

"A habit of mine," Kate said. "Now *you* must forgive *me*. How did a proper *sister* get involved with Professor Mandelbaum?"

Joan spread her legs straight out before her on the floor, in a position comfortable only to one whose body is in shape, a condition Kate found it subtly depressing to contemplate. Believing profoundly in the importance of athletics for women, of vigorous and aggressive games for girls, Kate herself had always shunned gym and all exercise, finding in walking the only physical exertion that did not strike her as ridiculous. Her slimness, like the greater part of her income, was inherited, not earned.

"How well do you know Harvard?" Joan asked.

"Not at all, for any intelligent purposes. I have attended graduations from time to time, family occasions being what they are. Assume vast ignorance."

"The administration of the English Department at Harvard is housed in one of those converted wooden buildings which Harvard has gradually bought up over the centuries and used for whatever purpose suited them. They own Cambridge, to all intents and purposes. This one once belonged to a guy named Warren, so they tell it, who had asthma or arthritis or something, and used to sit on his balcony, which was glass-enclosed because he couldn't stand humidity, and watch his guests disporting themselves. His house was supposed to have been a station for escaping slaves, but God knows what is true at Harvard and what is flattering legend. Anyway, the place is pretty much unreconstructed, the glass wall is still on the balcony, and on the second floor there's an ancient bathroom complete with mahogany bathtub, toilet with chain to pull from above, and a general air of being one of the first examples of elegant indoor plumbing. The shower still works; it had been turned on Janet. The room is now a ladies' rest room, partly because a female assistant professor occasionally crosses the threshold, not to mention female graduate students without whom none of these institutions could continue for a minute, but no doubt the real reason for its female assignment was the secretaries or, as I'm sure they're called, the girls."

"All right," Kate said. "I'm with you so far. Personally, I'd feel grateful to Harvard, if I lived in Cambridge, for not pulling down these old houses and erecting some glass and cement monstrosity in their place, but that's what makes me a member of the establishment and no sister, I suppose."

"You're getting the picture," Joan said. "They serve

their own purposes. Occasionally, these coincide with female purposes, but only very occasionally, and then by accident. Anyway, Janet Mandelbaum was found one evening in that mahogany-sided bathtub, stewed to the gills, zonked out, and immersed in water, all but her head. Luellen May, one of the sisters, was with her."

"With her?"

"Yes. A call came through to the coffee house that it was one of the sisters in the tub. Luellen went to see. It was a trap, of course."

"Did all this get much publicity?"

"No, Harvard sat on it, in their own interests. But there were lots of witnesses and the story got around, in the worst way."

"What does Janet say?"

"She says she doesn't know how she got there. No one believes her, other than that she got sloshed and passed out. Needless to say, for Professor Mandelbaum it's a terrible story, and the worst part is being associated in any way with Luellen. Our Janet doesn't even want to be associated with women graduate students."

"The story can't have got absolutely around," Kate said, "or I would have heard it."

"I bet your male colleagues have heard it. Would they be likely to tell it to you?"

Kate shook her head slowly. "One or two of them might, if they happened to be talking to me alone. What do you want me to do?"

"Janet wants you to come to Harvard and help her."

"It's odd," Kate said. "I only knew her when we were graduate students. Of course, we saw a great deal of each other then. Do you know Gertrude Stein? She said of her brother Leo, I think, 'We always had been together and now we were never at all together. Little by little we never met again.' When did she want me to come to Harvard?"

"I don't know; soon. After the Christmas holidays, maybe."

"And why are you, who despise Janet, bringing this message?"

"I thought, we all thought, that if you came to help Janet, we might get you to help Luellen. She's in a custody fight for her kids, and this isn't going to do her any good."

They sat a moment in silence, both staring at Jocasta, whose complete relaxation on the couch was disturbed only by the dreams of dogdom, revealed in racing feet.

"I know," Joan said, getting to her feet, "you'll have to think about it. Anyway, you may hear from Janet. Come on, Jocasta, you lazy bitch." The lazy bitch did not respond to this; then a piercing whistle from between Joan's teeth brought the dog's head up with a start.

"I've always wanted to whistle that way," Kate said. "Tell me this. If you would lie to any man, or any woman who works with men, and consider it your duty, why should I believe you?"

"You shouldn't," Joan said. "Check it out. Why not go up and check it out? We've got a pad, if you need one. Don't we, Jocasta?"

"Hampshire Street," Kate said. "I might want coffee."

"Maybe Next Time, the place is called. Ask anyone."

When they had gone, Kate absently picked some of Jocasta's white hairs off the couch. She rather wished she had a dog, but there was no way it could fit into her life, or Reed's. "Horse manure," she reminded herself, laughing. It was annoying to find Jocasta appealing, but even worse to respond to something attractive in Joan Theresa, who hated male institutions. "Sisters," Kate snorted. Then she went to the window. Below, Joan Theresa could be seen racing down the avenue, and Jocasta after her, as Joyce more or less said, with her lugs back for all she was bloody well worth.

Chapter 2

"OF COURSE," Mark Evergreen added, when the waiter
had filled their water glasses and left them to their Faculty Club Lunch, "he's gay. But you know that."

"So I have heard," Kate said. "Lively, merry, and
given to the wearing of bright colors; full of sprightly
activity."

"Oh dear," Mark said. "I ought not to have mentioned it so flatly. You are offended."

"Only by the word. I mourn for words. Clarissa Dalloway thought of Peter Walsh, 'If I had married him,
this gaiety would have been mine all day.' Could one
write that sentence now? It would evoke the kind of
snicker reminiscent of those occasions in my childhood
when one innocently referred to fairies. Perhaps, if gay
comes to mean homosexual, we shall recover fairies to
describe the wee folk, living at the bottom of my garden
or anywhere else."

"You have nothing against homosexuals as such?"

" 'As such.' Really, Mark, what a phrase! Language
apart, I welcome the changes of the seventies. Odd decades in our century seem to be ghastly, have you noticed, the thirties, the fifties, the seventies. Full of depressions, witch-hunts and dishonesty in high places.
Still, a lot of refreshing things happened in the seventies, including more honesty and sense about homosex-

uals. A charming friend, gay in all the marvelous sense of that word, confided to me, in keeping with the temper of the times, that he had come out of the closet. Now that's a phrase that makes no unwarranted claims upon the language—indeed, as a phrase, it's etymologically quite sound. The point is, he was just as nice, as good company, as trustworthy, as informed in the closet as out of it, and I found very little changed in him that I needed to take account of, except that he had usurped that lovely word gay. I could scarcely go around saying he was the gayest man I knew, which was the simple truth, and a high compliment into the bargain."

"Kate, is something wrong? I know you are given to off-the-cuff disquisitions, but you seem a bit more skittish than usual. What else can I tell you about Clarkville? I assume you know his work as well as I do."

"It's just that you know *him* better than I do, and I wondered . . ."

"You've heard about the Janet Mandelbaum in the bathtub brouhaha. I should have guessed."

"I haven't exactly *heard* of it; I was told. Do you know what happened, since you know Clarkville so well?"

"She got stewed and wet. Clarkville more or less suggested that the strain had been too much; I should think being the first tenured woman in the Harvard English Department would be a strain on Aphrodite, let alone Janet Mandelbaum. Apparently she got crocked, decided to take a bath and cool off, and passed out."

"Did you hear of anyone else being involved?"

"Some woman from around there, yes. Went apparently to the rescue, no one knows why. Janet firmly denies ever having set eyes on her, and the other woman concurs. Both, one gathers, emphatically and even insultingly. Are you worried about all this?"

"Mark, do you remember Janet Mandelbaum?"

"Do I not? Beauty *and* brains. And about as conventional and unimaginative as John Livingston Lowes, who counted every word Coleridge had ever read."

"Also from Harvard."

"Naturally. Her point, you will remember, is that to apply modern criticism to Donne and Herbert is as acceptable as to see Shakespeare as our contemporary. She collected contemporary hymn books, contemporary with Donne and Herbert, that is. I thought her the most boring woman I'd ever met, or would have if she weren't so absolutely alluring . . ."

His eyes, raised, met Kate's.

"She was not," Kate said, "very forthcoming. Or so one was to gather."

"Not very, no. Though even seventeenth-century scholars whose work she was lambasting drooled. We all yearned for you, of course, but . . ."

"Mark. It's been suggested that she has asked for me. Not directly, as it happens, but somehow in connection with this thing at Harvard. Does that seem to you a likely story? And how serious do you think this mess at Harvard is?"

"Second question first. If I were interested in women at Harvard, I would think it was damn serious. So I do. If I were like most of our male colleagues, I would find it laughable. I would snicker. First question second. Would Janet ask for you, indirectly of course? Directness was never Janet's line. Who else is there, Kate? Women your age—our age—who are professors in prestigious universities and know all about what that is like are not exactly legion. If, in addition, there is one such woman with whom you were in graduate school, with whom, in all those otherwise male bull sessions, you must have repaired to the ladies' room . . . yes, even Janet might think of her. You."

"Mark, if Harvard invited you to join their department, would you go?"

"Like a shot."

"Why?"

"I hate New York. Teaching at Harvard, I could live in the country and keep a boat."

"I love New York. I couldn't imagine spending one's life around Harvard Square, where everyone is so aggressively young."

"You might, however, consider paying it a visit. I hear they've moved that huge subway station in the middle of the square. You know, the one a Harvard newspaper said President Lowell was opposed to: 'President fights erection in Harvard Square' was, I believe, the disputed headline. It's no good trying not to smile; I know you think it's funny."

Certain events, as Kate was subsequently to write to Reed, are overdetermined: many causes apparently conspire to bring them about. One of these causes, a seasoned and witty woman, was waiting for Kate at a restaurant that evening. She was, as she said, on her way through from Washington. Kate had neglected to ask "through to where?" but she was not to be left wondering long.

"On my way to Harvard; leave of absence from my job. A consultant, if you can believe it, to the Government Department, or the Kennedy Center, or both. Talk about numerous birds with one stone: Harvard gets some practical advice *and* a woman they can point to statistically without being stuck with; I get a new experience and a chance to see what the hell goes on up there, not that I can't guess. George gets time to find out if what he really wants is to sail boats, write a novel or sleep with somebody's secretary, and my next in line in Washington gets a chance to practice a little power. What more could one ask?"

"Is George happy about it?"

"Kate, my dear, *entre nous* and all that, I don't madly care. I know the number of women to whom I could confess that could be added up by a two-toed sloth using half its equipment, but the fact is, well, I do care, of course, that's not the way to put it, but I don't sit around and stew. It's the clearest view of the male role I've ever had. I love George, and respond to discussions, requests and emergencies, but he isn't my whole life anymore. So have men ever felt about their wives. He wanted a chance to get off the treadmill, out of the rat race, to live by natural rhythms—you know.

And so he can. If he finds that his natural rhythms
don't suit him, there we are, aren't we? I've got a large
enough apartment for him to visit in Cambridge when
he chooses, and I recognize that what follows is *his*
problem. You may now stalk from the restaurant and
look for more womanly friends, up to their chins in
guilt. But do wait for the pasta, it's damn good."

"Have you noticed one's tendency lately to have all
one's conversations in restaurants? I think it's a new
sort of communion, bread, wine and a table. When
Reed is home, we do occasionally talk without con-
sumption; naturally, I talk to students and once in a
while even colleagues across a desk. Mostly, friends
these days share calories and courage simultaneously."

"What about you without Reed? Think how honest
I've been about George."

"Sylvia, you don't want me to compose stories of
marital disquiet for your delectation. Reed always knew
I had to have times without him. I always knew that he
never bored me when I was with him. He's a male
strangely composed: the pomposity was omitted.
Though I miss him, I don't pine for him when we're
apart, nor pine for solitude when we're together.
Greater tribute hath no woman."

"Solitude in marriage. What a joke. As I totter on
into advanced middle age, I've become aware of American marriage myths. My favorite at the moment is the
shared bedroom. Give that up, and you have given up
the marriage, all but the dry legalities. Friends in Washington—we play tennis, and she's waking up in her
quiet way—decided that they were constantly disturb-
ing each other's sleep; he snores, she arises during the
night, a habit she was loath to reform by taking no liq-
uids after eight P.M., and it came to them in one of
those intense moments of illumination that, since they
had plenty of rooms, why not sleep separately? You'd
think they'd decided to be tattooed, or run guns to
Cuba. What would people think? They finally solved
the problem by placing a large sign over one of the bedroom doors: *We Fuck Here*."

"I've missed you, Sylvia."

"Of course you have. Why not desert that male institution of yours for the even more male institution on the Charles? You can share my large apartment, when George isn't there."

"What do I do when he *is* there?"

"You take a set of rooms in one of the houses, and repair to the company of undergraduates and Fellows' sherry while I cavort matrimonially."

"We haven't mentioned what I'm doing at Harvard, not to ask how I get the set of rooms in one of the houses."

"I'm a woman of influence, haven't you been listening? I know Kennedys and people who know Kennedys, and when I talk, people listen."

"Well, I'm listening all right, but let me remind you that this semester isn't over, and I have to teach next. One has a contract, little as some of one's colleagues notice it."

"Nonsense. You take a semester's leave without pay. They'll be overjoyed; think of the money they'll save, half your annual salary. If one of your courses is absolutely necessary, they'll hire some unemployed genius to teach it for a fifth of your salary. I've worked it all out, Kate; you're rich, thank God. Off you go to that Institute they've got up there for women scholars, stay with me, and go to the aid of Janet Mandelbaum."

"So we have come at last to Janet Mandelbaum. What a coincidence."

"Not a coincidence; a concatenation perhaps."

"Before you explain *that,* a few questions, if you don't mind. Why should this Institute for female scholars take me? Surely they're full to overflowing by now."

"Always room for one more, when the right people ask. In fact, they can't give nearly as many fellowships as they'd like, but if you come, as the English say, with the honor but without the emoluments, they'll find you a study, give you a mailbox, call you a Fellow, and require that you give a lecture on the subject of your endeavors. What about it? The Institute will be fine;

you'll see. Staying in a house will be a little more sticky. You'll have to swear to go to all the Fellows' lunches, preceded by sherry and followed by spiritual indigestion, but you'll be doing it for the good of womanhood."

"Sylvia, what am I doing for the good of womanhood?"

"Saving Janet, of course, and the cause of female professors at Harvard. She's being framed, I'm certain."

"Framed?"

"You heard me. If you don't agree, find out for yourself. Between us, my dear, when the patriarchy gets worried, it goes into action, with money and all that money can buy. Did you know that the Mormon Church gave fifteen million dollars in one year to defeat the Equal Rights Amendment?"

"Sylvia! You're becoming one of those awful women's libbers!" Kate said with mock horror.

"You betcha. I eat bras; my favorite is 34B, pink, lightly sizzled. I will eat one soon if the waiter doesn't come. Shall we have it with white wine or red?"

The waiter, perhaps to forestall this, arrived full of eager attention, and during dinner they spoke in a desultory manner of many things. It was only over the Irish coffee, which Sylvia had, without much difficulty, persuaded Kate to indulge in, that Kate returned to her possible visit to Harvard.

"Sylvia, I may go to Harvard, or I may not, but I'm not even going to send Janet Mandelbaum a friendly postcard, unless you tell me why you think she's being framed. Why, in fact, this is all so important?"

"How much do you know about these new chairs at Harvard?"

"Little enough; nothing really."

"It's not the first time, you know, that women have been so honored. Over thirty years ago, the Zemurray-Stone Professorship was established at Harvard. It's been continuously filled, so far, by three occupants,

since 1948.* The Professorship has probably been a
success, as professorships go, but it hasn't turned out to
do much for women as a whole. The first incumbent
was a Scotswoman: naturally Harvard couldn't find a
qualified American woman, and at least if they had to
have a woman, they could make sure she came from
abroad. All reports suggest that this woman, Helen
Cam, a historian, was a gem, and the committee that
chose her did include a woman, which is more than the
committee that chose poor Janet did. Not only a good
scholar and a good friend, Cam was a good person generally: she soon got permission to attend Harvard
Morning Prayers, though she was the first female to do
so since daily prayers had been instituted in 1638."

"Was she the first Harvard woman professor?"

"No. I think women were always called lecturers
even when they knew more than everyone else in sight,
as in astronomy, but Dr. Alice Hamilton was made an
Assistant Professor in the Medical School. I think they
had no choice, since she had invented the field of in-
dustrial medicine; anyway, she was certainly its out-
standing practitioner, even Harvard could see that. But
each year she would get an invitation to the Commencement Exercises with a handwritten addendum: 'Ladies are not permitted to march in the procession.' She
also agreed, I think, not to take up her faculty rights to
football tickets. Alice Hamilton, by the way, lived to be
ninety-five and to publicly oppose the Vietnam War.
But I must keep to my point. Once one starts with
women at Harvard, one can easily be tempted from the
proper pathway. Where was I?"

"Helen Cam from Scotland."

"Ah, yes. After Cam retired, the chair was filled by
Cora Du Bois, an anthropologist, famous for her study

---

*For information about the Zemurray-Stone Professorship, the
reader is urged to consult an unpublished (but available at
Harvard) article on the founding of the professorship by Bernice
Brown Cronkhite, whose idea it largely was. Sylvia has clearly
read this article.

of the people of Alor, an island in the Dutch East In-
dies. When she retired, the present incumbent was appointed; she's not *that* much older than thee and me.
Her field is classics, and she's just published some
widely admired book, on Greek art, I think. A first-rate
scholar."

"But is she particularly interested in the cause of
women as such? That's a new phrase I've picked up: as
such."

"Whether she is or not, one professorship clearly
wasn't going to accomplish what the Zemurray-Stone
may have intended: more regard for women professors
at Harvard. Anyway, someone—who is the best-kept
secret in years—has endowed this woman's chair, and
threatens to endow others. I say threatens because
that's how some people look at it, I think."

"You think someone has set out to sabotage it?"

"I do, but since I've always sneered at conspiracy
theories, I shall resist the temptation to develop one.
Say it's not a conspiracy, it's just one lunatic. I still
think Janet Mandelbaum needs help. And she has
asked for you."

"So everyone says. The last time I saw her, years
ago, there wasn't awfully much for us to talk about."

"I suspect she may have more to talk about now,
Kate; think of it, she's such a sitting duck. Once the
male club refuses to support its special female members, where has she to turn? Harvard isn't offering support. They don't even offer much support to new or visiting professors of the right sex, from what I've heard.
Janet doesn't want the support of feminists, and can't expect it. She must be feeling pretty cornered."

"So she turns to companions from the past, even a
past lived in a different world?"

"I think so. At least you'll know what she's talking
about. And of course she's upset by being connected
with the women from that commune. Don't tell me *that*
wasn't a plot."

"I've met one of those women from the commune,

did you know? Complete with marvelous bullterrier. They came all the way to New York to invite me."

"What did you think of her? The woman, I mean."

"She said she was a sister, and I liked her, I'm afraid."

"Why afraid?"

"Because they are willing enough to use me. Comes the revolution, I'll be the first to go."

"We have a little time to wait, I think. Meanwhile, the sisters are the biggest mistake *they* made, whoever *they* are."

"Mistake?"

"Kate dear, use your brain. There was no way those women, outside the institutions and in a commune, were going to come to the aid of straight women. Straight women work with the oppressor, are male-identified, and tend toward male lovers."

"Sylvia, does one's sex life have to come into this inevitably?"

"Inevitably. The point, however, is that *they* thought they could discredit Janet by getting her involved with that all-women commune in Cambridge. Perhaps add another suspicion to her deteriorating reputation. But they were fools. They united two groups who would never, otherwise, have anything to do with each other: the woman-identified and the male-identified."

"Well, I absolutely refuse to consider myself either," Kate said.

"I know, my dear, that's why we need you. But don't forget, you live with a man, you work with men, you support the patriarchal institutions."

Kate raised a brandy glass that had appeared before her. "Didn't a patriarchal institution invent brandy?"

"The women who run the coffee house in Cambridge will probably tell you that women, who cared for the vines and grapes, invented it, and men usurped both the credit and the brandy. They're probably right, but don't let anyone hear you say it."

"I think I like Joan Theresa better than Janet Mandelbaum."

"That, my dear, is one of the problems. And you must never say so while having sherry in the Senior Common Room in whatever Harvard House you end up."

"How do I get in touch with your women's institute at Radcliffe, supposing I go along with this preposterous plan?"

"I'll arrange it all. Leave it to Sylvia, who is she, that all the swains obey her? I'll send you a nice fat packet about women at Harvard. It's a particularly depressing collection of materials. First, Harvard never thought there was a problem. Then, when about a hundred years later they saw there was one, they set up a commission and wrote a report about it. Quite a good report. And then nothing happened. Or nothing much."

"What about Radcliffe? No help from there?"

"My dear, Radcliffe was started by accident, and has never been seen as anything but a convenience to Harvard. A woman who grew up in Cambridge has just written a book about her youth. She says the experiment of Radcliffe College, which was originally called the Harvard Annex, naturally, 'was to be tried by a few ladies who were quite unorganized, so that if failure should be the result, Harvard would not be responsible, though if success should crown the effort, Harvard should have the glory.' That sums up Harvard-Radcliffe relations. The 'ladies' are still quite unorganized."

"Do you know why I shall probably come to Cambridge, much as I loathe Harvard Square?" Kate asked. "Because it will so thoroughly and delightfully upset my brothers, who don't think Harvard should ever have let women wander around Widener Library. Come to think of it, I've got a niece who must have graduated from Radcliffe recently. Well, I look forward to seeing Jocasta again."

"Janet Mandelbaum, beware! Rescue is on the way."

Chapter 3

<hr>

It has been many years since women graduate students were forbidden to enter the Widener stacks, and Margaret Mead's story of a female graduate student in physical anthropology who had to sit in a closet and listen to lectures through a crack in the door is now an amusing anecdote in the social history of past decades.
REPORT OF THE COMMITTEE ON THE
STATUS OF WOMEN IN THE FACULTY
OF ARTS AND SCIENCES

SYLVIA, who seemed to be engrossed in a matrimonial interlude, had reserved a room for Kate at the Harvard Faculty Club for a few days. Nowhere has it been demonstrated that the Harvard Faculty Club saves the worst rooms for women unattached by blood or marriage to Harvard Overseers or Trustees. The only clear fact is that Kate, despite Sylvia's advance notice to the Club, was given an attic room with a dormer window, no closet, only one electric outlet to which had to be attached, seriatim, the room's only lamp, its radio, and the device that brought water to a temperature almost sufficient to dissolve the unspeakable instant coffee provided in small packets. Kate, staring about her, decided that no room could be that uncomfortable and inconvenient by accident. The degree of casual malevolence pointed to a sinister mind at work. Kate was, in any case, prepared to suppose that Harvard's general attitudes toward women were not badly represented by this room.

The room's only window, and only source of natural light, was in a dormer extending out at least six feet from the room itself. Nor was air available at the end of this narrow passage, for a sign in the window stated peremptorily: *These windows have been sealed for the winter. Please use the air conditioner if ventilation is required.* Since ventilation had been required long since, Kate turned on the air conditioner. She was provided with a gentle draft of stale air and noise, both frightful; Kate turned both off. Peering over the air conditioner, she contemplated the beautiful trees which shook in a January wind. One might as well admire the natural beauties of Harvard which were, admit it, many. At that moment, so still was she standing, a squirrel raced along the gutter and came to a stop on the sill just outside. It removed from its cheek a large nut and placed it carefully between the strips of steel on the sill, patting it into place. A gift, perhaps, Kate thought when the squirrel had gone, from what Hardy called the Great Mother. A better omen for her Harvard escapade than this dreary room. Somewhat cheered, she set out to explore Harvard and Cambridge, before meeting Sylvia in the Club's cocktail lounge at five.

From her attic window Kate had been able to see Warren House, within whose walls Janet had met her odd fate. She now crossed beneath the beautiful trees and entered the building. To her left, out of sight, secretaries, or at any rate typists, pursued their noisy tasks. To her right was a closed door bearing a notice: *Placement Officer.* Kate shuddered in sympathy. She too had served as placement officer in those bad times when jobs were scarce even, she supposed, for Harvard Ph.D.'s. Quickly, before anyone emerged to ask her what she wanted, she mounted the stairs to the second floor. There, behind an open door, stood the famous living room of the asthmatic or arthritic Mr. Warren. His glass wall was still in place on the balcony. Down the hall from this was the ancient, dignified bathroom. Nature's very functions seemed more stately contemplated before all this mahogany. On the door was tacked a small card: *Ladies' Rest Room. Men's Room on First Floor.*

Warren House contained little more than the Chairman's Office, the Placement Office, and meeting rooms. For all its charm and antique mahogany, it was the center of Harvard English Department might and, deserted though it was, spoke loudly of long-held power and patriarchal attitudes. Suddenly, Kate recognized that her mood needed airing; she left the building, crossed Quincy Street with a sigh of relief and headed for a bookstore. What she wanted was a good browse. The bookstores around Harvard offered the book lover a rare opportunity to indulge the art of browsing; unlike most New York bookstores, they had large collections of books on every subject, not just those titles published to great hoopla in the last six months.

Kate began with the Coop, as the Harvard Cooperative Society called itself. Ignoring the best sellers on the first floor, she stepped onto the escalator to be carried upward toward the paperbacks, only to find herself hailed by an eccentric figure floating downward on the adjoining escalator.

"Aunt Kate!" this creature called. "What on earth are you doing *here?*" for all the world, Kate thought, as though she had appeared as the protagonist in a massage parlor. She stared with some fascination at her niece, if it *was* her niece, and was in consequence bounced off the escalator when it had achieved its purpose of carrying her to the second floor. Her niece as might be, wearing a floating cloak or cape, its hood pulled forward over her face, the whole covering blue jeans and (presumably) the inevitable T-shirt, leaped off the down escalator and onto the up with all the agility of a witch on a broomstick, which indeed she rather resembled. Not for her the slow ascent of the escalator. Bounding up the treads she arrived panting beside her aunt, whom she regarded with an expression of such joy, and eventually hugged with such vigor, that Kate, in spite of herself, collapsed into what someone had once called her most attractive "auntilary" attitudes. "How are you, my dear?" she rather breathlessly inquired.

"Fine. Fine. But how absolutely extraordinary to find you here, I mean of all people, so absolutely New York. Why didn't you tell me you were coming? Do the parents know? I suppose not, you never tell them anything, or so they claim. *Are* you going to teach at Harvard, Kate, what fun, I'll get everybody to come and applaud. No one applauds much at Harvard, they're far too sophisticated. Often they hiss."

During this monologue, Kate and her niece (whose first name was something *far* too ordinary, and who called herself, and was called by everyone except her parents, Leighton, which either was or was not her mother's maiden name; Kate was really most unreliable about her relatives) were being shoved and pushed and stared at by the not inconsiderable traffic on the second floor of the Coop.

"You look exhausted," Leighton said. "I know, you want a drink. Let's go," and she rather edged her aunt toward the down escalator. "I'm learning to drink at last, it's been such a bore acting like a puritan because I loathed the stuff. You have a martini, isn't that what you always drink, and I'll have a sombrero."

"The cocktail lounge at the Faculty Club doesn't open until five," Kate said, this time leaving the escalator under her own power and feeling, not uncommonly for those who find themselves in the vicinity of Harvard Square, a hundred-and-two-years old, "and as a matter of fact I've arranged . . ."

"We'll go to One Potato Two Potato," Leighton said. "Follow me!"

Their pace, though frantic, permitted thought rather than conversation and allowed Kate to dredge up such information about her niece as she in fact possessed. It wasn't much. Kate did not especially care for families, and especially did not care for hers. Her parents had long since departed for that special heaven to which they had always been certain their high birth and infallible rectitude entitled them, and her three brothers, all considerably older than she, had produced children who were, with only certain notable exceptions, as dull or as narrow as they. Leighton, of course, must be the last of the lot of the middle brother. In fact, she vaguely remembered sending an appropriate gift, cash, when the child graduated from the Theban. That she had gone to Harvard like all the other Fanslers except her nephew Leo, Kate took for granted. In her, Kate's, day, proper ladies did not go to Radcliffe unless they lived around the place. Today, presumably, any girl who could, went to what had come to be known as Harvard and Radcliffe Colleges, and if she was a Fansler, Harvard and Radcliffe greeted her application with a tolerant, not to say anticipatory, eye.

"I trust," Leighton said, when they had achieved One Potato etcetera, where Kate very much doubted they would know how to make a martini for which it was, in any case, far too early, "that you have money because I don't. Forgive me for saying that so bluntly, but it seemed better than having a gruesome scene when the check arrived."

"What did you intend to use for money in the Coop?" Kate asked, in what she hoped was a properly stern manner. This whole caper was bad enough without the addition of a niece. Surely the girl ought to have graduated by now. Kate distinctly remembered that her gift had been more than four years ago. Perhaps, she sadly concluded, time tended to telescope as one grew older.

"Oh, nobody uses *money* at the Coop," Leighton said, as though Kate had suggested wampum. "A sombrero, please," Leighton said to the hovering waitress, as she flung off her cape whose ends trailed, Kate could not help noticing, all over the floor. The waitress, shifting slightly westward, immediately stepped on it. Neither of them noticed. "And a very dry martini?" Leighton asked Kate.

"Yes, please." Kate was too defeated even to name her gin. "What," she asked when the waitress had departed, "is a sombrero? I ask though every instinct warns me not to."

"Kahlúa and milk. Very nourishing and delicious. I haven't had breakfast."

"And, naturally, you never eat lunch."

"Naturally. I diet until six when, overcome by self-satisfaction and starvation, I eat steadily until four A.M. It's very demoralizing. Aunt Kate—I think of you as *Aunt* Kate, though I'll try not to call you Aunt to your face, I do hope you don't find it offensive—why wasn't I created slim and tall and soignée like you? Really, genes are too perverse."

"I am *not* soignée."

"Well, right now you're rather hot and irritable, naturally, but mostly you're cool and elegant and intellectual and my absolute one and only role model. I've told everybody. I shall be a Professor of English and read poetry magnificently. Well, probably I'll be an actress, but that's just because there aren't any jobs for English professors anymore. You are still my model."

The arrival of the drinks (Kate's surprisingly good) happily prevented Kate's response to this barrage. She lit a cigarette. The combined effects of tobacco and gin enabled her to act more like an aunt. "What year are you in?" she asked.

"I'm a senior," Leighton said. "But I dropped out for a couple of years to act and sort of fool around, so I should have graduated two years ago. I'm majoring in Greek, I live in South House, I think Harvard education stinks, but I expect the name to help me get a job, and I spend most of my time around the Loeb Theater, just to get all the usual questions out of the way. Don't think I'm rude, but I'd really rather talk about important matters. Don't you think all this exchange of vital data is a bit insincere and boring, actually? If not, ask away."

Kate did think so, actually, though at the moment no question about Harvard was quite so insincere or boring as Leighton might imagine. Kate felt cheered, however, by discovering that her memory had not telescoped time, and that her niece had not, in fact, graduated from Harvard unnoticed by her aunt or, equally regrettable, failed to graduate.

"Why Greek?" Kate asked.

"Well, I learned Greek at the Theban. It's one of those subjects you can learn by memorizing everything forty-eight hours before the exam. That way, I pass the course and concentrate on what I like, which is acting and writing plays. I'm writing one now; I'm in Harvard's famous playwriting course."

"Famous for its students who later became famous?"

"Famous for its teacher, as far as I'm concerned. He's the nicest, most unpompous, kindest most un-Harvard person. We meet in Warren House, actually, where that woman professor got sloshed. *Kate!* Is *that* why you're here?"

"I suppose everyone knows about that little caper?" Kate sadly asked.

"Actually, it's made her more endearing, if you want to know. Talk about people with pokers up their asses . . ."

"Which, as far as I know, we weren't."

"Sorry. I keep forgetting I ought to treat you with more discretion."

"Not discretion. Decorum, perhaps. No, not decorum. Standard English, the Theban variety, the Theban variety for public occasions," Kate explained, referring to the school they had both, in their turn, attended. "Your reference to pokers suggests, I am to gather, that Professor Mandelbaum is not forthcoming."

"You *do* put it better. Might I have another sombrero? I've got a rehearsal in ten minutes. Well, actually I'm late already, but I don't come on until the second scene. *Hedda Gabler*. Now that, if you think about it, is what Professor Mandelbaum is like—Hedda, scared sh—scared to death of being unconventional but seething underneath. At least, Hedda might not have seethed at Harvard. Do you think I'm on to something?"

Leighton had caught the eye of the waitress and signaled a repeat. "I think I see what you mean," Kate said. "A not unfamiliar position for women today. They dislike the lot of the ordinary woman, but fear to eschew the proprieties of ordinary womanhood. I think that's rather a perceptive remark."

"Do you always use words like 'eschew'?"

"From time to time. Good heavens, talk about time, I shall be late meeting my five o'clock appointment and sloshed into the bargain, as you so delightfully put it."

Leighton, following what she clearly took to be a hint, downed her second sombrero and rose to her feet in one unbroken movement. "Kate, it's been wonderful. I think you're marvelous. Now don't worry that I shall haunt your footsteps and door, I shan't. But if you begin to be heard of, the name will of course be seen as the same as mine, or mine as yours, and you shall have either to claim or disown me. I do hope the decision will not disturb your sleep. Many thanks for the refreshment." She departed, flinging her hood over her head, and leaving Kate to wonder whether a flair for the dramatic would ever again be confined to the stage. Still, she had to admit, sipping only a small part of her second martini, the Fansler niece had turned out better than might have been expected. She might even be useful. The Fansler genes, Kate decided, thinking also of a favorite nephew, were looking up in the next generation. On the other hand, she sadly concluded, paying the bill and remembering her mission, the Fansler genes were looking like trouble in the only female member of her generation, her.

"My God," Sylvia said, greeting Kate in the cocktail lounge of the Faculty Club, "you can't have started already; it's only five. How's your room?"

"I shall forbear," Kate said, dropping into a chair, "describing my room. Let me say only that the sooner I leave it, the likelier I am to develop an objective view of Harvard. I left my room this afternoon, actually, only to find a niece. *Hedda Gabler* and Greek, with a flowing cape. Do you think I could have a glass of soda water?"

"Cheer up, my dear," said Sylvia, signaling for the soda water. "George departs tomorrow at dawn. Now that I think of it, George always departs at dawn. It's one of his nicest characteristics. So you may join me, with a bedroom and bath of your own: all the best modern conveniences. In the second place, Janet Mandelbaum is having dinner with you tomorrow night, at Ferdinand's. She thinks she is having dinner with the two of us, but I shall develop an emergency. I'll reserve a table for you, however. Third, the Institute is prepared to welcome you the morning after that. You can spend the days in between exploring Warren House."

"I have already explored Warren House. What House am I to be a Fellow of?"

"Dunster. Rather far away, I'm afraid, but musical. I thought you might like the concerts."

"Why does Dunster House think I'm here?"

"Dunster House does not think. It simply absorbs whatever comes its way, like a vacuum cleaner. The Masters think you are here at the Institute, which you are. Institute Fellows often get attached to Houses."

"Why Masters plural?"

"Women's liberation, my love, a move toward equal rights. Naturally, Masters' wives, like the wives of the clergy and politicians, worked twice as hard as their husbands who always had more important things to do, but got none of the credit not to mention money. Now husbands and wives are considered Co-Masters and sometimes, though rarely, the woman is the Master. I've got your faculty card, by the way." Sylvia produced a square of plastic which would entitle Kate to everything from the libraries to the squash courts.

"Sylvia, your preparations are so impressive that you fill me with trepidation. Or, as Leighton would say . . ."

"Who is Leighton?"

"My niece."

"Kate, this may be the greatest thing you ever did for

womanhood, for education, for Janet Mandelbaum, and to screw Harvard—if that's what Leighton would say."

Later, as she and Sylvia climbed the stairs to the first floor, a young man beckoned to her from the registration desk.

"Professor Fansler?"

Kate admitted it.

"These were left for you," he said. "I'll be sorry to part with them." "These" were a vase of carnations, white with red streaks on their blossoms; they looked and smelled lovely. A card was attached. Kate read it while the young man and Sylvia waited. *From your grateful niece. Good luck. Don't end up in any bathtubs.*

"Apparently," Kate said, half to herself, "one doesn't need money to buy flowers either." Having bid goodbye to Sylvia, she walked back to the elevator, thinking how much the flowers would do for that dreadful room. Flowers and a nut, Kate thought. Not bad, considering it's Harvard.

Chapter 4

Often women who have been assaulted by a friend or acquaintance feel uncertain about asking for help. Don't.
UNIVERSITY HEALTH SERVICE

THE NEXT EVENING, at Ferdinand's, Kate sipped a smaller and altogether more ladylike martini made with Beefeater gin, and faced Janet Mandelbaum for the first time in at least ten years. They chattered. Well, of course they chattered, that was what people did when they met after a long interval and a separation born of divergent views. In fact, Kate realized with a start, she had never liked Janet at all, and probably Janet had never liked her. Yet Kate had genuinely admired Janet's scholarship, Kate thought to herself, while Janet, with that attitude of natural superiority peculiar to those devoted to the earlier centuries of English literature, considered Kate's achievements as frivolous. One read novels, one didn't study them, not if one was serious. And Janet had been nothing if not serious. Except beautiful. Her seriousness was unchanged, her beauty perhaps transformed into prim, carefully coiffured good looks. Kate rather wondered what there was, beyond chatter, to be said.

It was surely a comment on the loneliness of Janet's life that Kate should have occurred to her as a friend; perhaps there is a certain youthful time when companionship, however superficial or circumstantial, confers a deeper bond of affection and trust than later meetings. Still, it would never have occurred to Kate to call upon

Janet, or perhaps it was more honest to say that Kate at the moment could not conceive of the circumstances where Janet's support, if available, would be helpful.

Janet waited for Kate to peruse the menu; she seemed, indeed, reluctant to begin, and mentioned Sylvia's absence. "I suspect," she said, "that she thought we ought to be alone together. I'm sorry for you; I'm not very good company these days."

"There are those who would think you should be on top of the world. After all, it's quite an achievement, isn't it, to be a professor at Harvard? You've accomplished the highest, at least in the world's view, in the academic marketplace."

"I thought so at first. But all the women—students, assistant professors, administrators—seem to think I should rally to some woman's cause: women's studies, the problems of women at Harvard, welcoming women to the graduate program, to Radcliffe—as though there were only one sex in the universe. Why should I be more interested in the women than the men? I'm interested in good seventeenth-century scholars; the sex is irrelevant. The soft-shelled crabs are very good; frozen, but good. I've had them before."

"Janet, you must have guessed if you were coming to Harvard that the fact of your being a woman would not be irrelevant. Despite your high qualifications, and those of other women scholars in the past, none has been hired at Harvard before."

"I inquired into the Zemurray-Stone Professorship— do you know about that?" Kate nodded. "No one expected those women to do anything but their job; they were hired to be what they were, historians, anthropologists, whatever."

"Those were different times."

Janet tore a roll apart with some vigor. "I will *not* say 'chairperson.' I think that's a revolting term. I will not destroy every sentence with him/her, he/she, or other nonsense. I honestly do think that if women have the ability and are willing to pay the price they can make it. I did. You did."

She had actually said it. She needed, desperately needed, to believe that the times had nothing to do with it: she had been chosen because she deserved to be chosen, and had simply been overlooked earlier. Kate wanted to speak; she sensed the dark trouble this woman was in and knew that kindness lay in speaking. But even as Kate sought a neutral topic, Janet, with a great gulp, started crying, and was clearly not going to be able to stop. She snorted into her napkin and dripped into her pâté. Kate waved to the waiter, proffered a charge card, explained that her friend had been taken ill, and in a remarkably short time found herself walking with Janet Mandelbaum along Mount Auburn Street. The night was cold, and Janet blew her nose in the napkin which she had carried away from Ferdinand's. It was a mark of how completely Kate veered between two worlds that she found herself wondering if Janet would remember to return it. "You," a young feminist had once said to Kate, "are from another planet, like, I mean, out of this world." Where napkins are returned, Kate thought. I need a drink.

The drink, when Kate returned with Janet to the apartment on Mount Auburn Street she shared with Sylvia (who appeared to have gone out in pursuit of her emergency), was easier to acquire than Janet's quiescence. Leaving her to her gradually subsiding tears, Kate went in search of sustenance and returned with crackers and cheese. She doubted Janet would want them, but Kate had great faith in filtering alcohol through substance; anyhow, she was hungry.

Clearly, it was going to be a long evening. No doubt the whole thing would turn out to be a mare's nest. (Now where had that phrase come from? Kate had acquired a dictionary of clichés, compiled by Eric Partridge, but he had a disconcerting way of saying what the cliché meant, which Kate knew, and not how it arose, which she wondered. Kate brought her mind firmly back to Harvard.) The apartment they were sitting in had floor-to-ceiling windows looking over the

Charles River. In the mornings, very early, as Kate
would soon discover, crews from all the colleges
around, and they were many, practiced, the cox shouting with a vigor suited to his task but not to the slumber
of others. Nonetheless, the view was worth anything.
There was something about rivers. Kate decided to
switch from alcohol to coffee, and excused herself to go
into the kitchen and make it. Pray God it *was* a mare's
nest.

When she returned, Janet had somewhat quieted
down. She did not apologize, for which Kate was grateful. In fact, she was mildly accusatory. "I don't know
why I wanted to see you," she said. "We were in the
same crowd in the old days, and I thought you would
be in the same situation, if you see what I mean. You
were always so . . ."

"Establishment?"

"Yes, I guess so. And I can't believe that you believe
in women's studies. No one has ever talked about men's
studies." Janet was working herself up again. Kate decided to be firm.

"Janet, I think we shall get further if we try not to
argue about feminism. That is, I'll be glad to argue by
the hour, if you really want to, after tonight, but for
now, why not tell me what you thought I might have
been able to help you with, if I had been the sort of
person you thought I was?"

"Before I was hired, some of the professors in the
department here had me to dinner, and so on; they
were welcoming, and everything seemed so civilized.
But once I got here, actually to work, I found myself
rather isolated. Oh, there's certainly enough to do
around Harvard, every night of the year, and I had
plenty of work, and the young women in the various
departments invited me out, but . . ."

"Not the men. They're courteous enough, if they
meet you in passing, but not what you'd call friendly."

"That's it. And then I got a note, on department sta-
tionery, saying there would be a party in the living

room at Warren House, you know, with the glass balcony . . ."

"I've seen it," Kate said. "A nice room for a party."
But, she thought to herself, pity Janet wasn't watching
it from behind the glass-enclosed balcony, like the
house's original owner.

"When I got there, there were all young people. Both
sexes, nicely dressed. I thought the older professors
came later; one never knows the customs at Harvard. I
was offered a drink by a pleasant young man. That's
the last thing I remember."

"Until?"

"I woke up, in the bathtub, full of water, and this
woman, this . . . she was saying, 'Who the fuck are
you?' And then some young men came up and found
us, and one of them said, 'It looks as though we know
the sort she is, all right.' All, all those women, he
meant, are the same. They're . . ."

"Dykes?" Kate harshly said.

"Yes." Janet began to weep again.

"Janet, is that bothering you still? You've been a
professor for years, maybe not at Harvard, but in a university. What did you think men said about women like
us, particularly unmarried women? When we were
graduate students we had balls, and now we're lesbians.
You can't still be bothered about that."

"I am bothered. I can't even bring myself to say the
words you say."

"They count on that, my dear."

"I think those, those women in overalls and boots are
horrible."

"But I dare say," Kate wickedly argued against all
her firm resolutions, "that you rather like gay men: so
debonair, so gracious, so useful as escorts. Oh, Janet,
sit down, I'm sorry. Please sit down. Whatever your
views, or mine, one thing is clear: it was a frame-up.
They not only saw to it that you were found drunk and
wet, but in the company of a radical feminist from a
commune. They seem to have hit all the panic buttons

at once. The question, of course, is who did it. And why."

"Why is obvious, I should have thought. To discredit me."

"Yes, my dear, but why? Is it a personal grudge against you, a grudge against women at Harvard, women as professors at important universities, women at large? Or was it just a naughty prank? They meant to discourage you and make you ashamed, but were they trying to discourage *you*, the donor of your chair, Harvard or the women's movement? And who, I need hardly add, are *they?*"

"Do you think I could have a drink after all?" Janet asked.

"Scotch? It gives you cancer, by the latest reports."

"That might be a pleasant relief." Janet tried to collect herself. "Campari and soda, if you have it." She waited for her drink before speaking. "You know something, Kate, I never really liked you. But I wanted to. You seemed so sure of yourself, so . . ."

"If you say soignée, I shall hit you, I promise."

"I resented you, that's the truth. I don't know why I thought you could help me. But none of the women professors here seemed exactly approachable, or else they were libbers themselves and obviously assumed I was, and their . . ."

"Janet, listen. I keep interrupting you and saying, 'Janet, listen.' Do listen. I am now here. Sylvia is now here. We will try to comfort you, we can be consulted, we promise not to argue feminism, if you'll at least try not to sound like Phyllis Schlafly on one of her more histrionic days. Consult us, talk to us, let us help you. We'll try to find out what's going on. But, and I know it's a big but, you've got to carry on as though nothing had happened. Nothing. You've got looks, and dignity, and poise and a hell of a great reputation as a scholar, and you're going to have to use every ounce of all those things. I know it seems unlikely now, but this will pass. And you haven't really got a choice, you know, unless you want to take early retirement and go into partnership with Marabel Morgan. You're not going to be exactly sought after by other universities unless you live this down. So hang in there, as the young so monstrously say, and let us help as much as we can."

"But how did I get into the bathtub?"

"My dear, I take it you always drink Campari and soda. There could be *anything* in Campari and soda. There was something in your Campari and soda. Would you like another now, by the way?"

The next day Kate was greeted at the Institute as to another world. Here at least women were not problematic. If Harvard ignored them, they tended to return the compliment, practicalities apart. Kate was shown her office, the meeting room for Fellows, kitchens, all the amenities. Her immediate response was a desire to shut herself up in her office and plunge into some scholarly work—something to do, perhaps, with the habits of minor molecules. She did, of course, have a project, and would be required to lecture on it during the semester. But Kate found herself barely able even to recall her subject.

Left in her office, Kate seated herself in the armchair provided and went off into a kind of trance. Just outside her window was a beautiful old elm. Even as she looked out at the Radcliffe Yard, snow began to fall. Kate put her feet on the desk chair, gazed with pleasure at the quiet, collegiate scene, and let her thoughts chase each other through her mind.

She and Sylvia had been up until all hours, as Kate's mother used to say, talking about Janet who had, upon Sylvia's return, been dispatched home in a taxi. Kate had even admitted to wondering if Janet might not have had a brainstorm and got herself into the bath, who knew why or how.

"I thought of that myself," Sylvia had said. "You know how unstable women are, particularly when the maternal instinct has been thwarted. But how does that explain the woman from the commune? Someone called her. Someone, furthermore, who knew enough to get

her there by mentioning a sister. Kate, I wouldn't want
to say this to anyone else, but do you think the separa-
tist women are trying to undermine the establishment
women and the plot went awry? Well, neither do I, but
I feel we are constrained to think of everything. And so
brainwashed have we been by the patriarchy that I'd
sooner blame a group of women than a Harvard professor, though Lord knows they are as likely as anyone to
go bonkers, and likelier than most. Did you hear about
the one who absolutely insisted upon his seventeenth-
century right to graze a cow on the Cambridge common, keeping it, meanwhile, in his living room? Well, I
don't believe that either, but it just goes to show,
doesn't it?"

What it went to show Kate might have thought out,
watching the snow and the elm tree, had there not been
a knock on her door. "Come in," Kate called, expecting, though she was not sure on what errand, a female.

But the figure that entered was male, rather, given
Kate's state of mind, overwhelmingly so. He had been
in graduate school with her and was, in fact, the first
man she had ever slept with, that occasion not having
been notably great, but the subsequent ones . . . the
point, Kate sternly reminded herself, being that he had
married not Kate, but Janet.

"Moon!" Kate said, finding her voice. "What in
God's name are you doing here?"

"Is the emphasis on you, here, or doing?" Moon
asked. He came in and closed the door behind him.
"May I sit?" he asked. Kate looked at him and her
heart turned over. Well, she admitted to herself, not her
heart exactly. The fact is, Kate said to herself, rather
helplessly . . .

"The accent is on here," she said to Moon. "Here, at
Harvard, at Radcliffe, in my study. Here."

"I teach writing. Read in the *Gazette* you were coming as a Fellow of this place. So I wandered over and
asked and here you are. How are you, Kate?"

"I could be better," Kate said. "In certain ways, I've

never been worse. I'm in a mess, I don't know how I got into it, and I don't know how to get out."

"That's almost the first thing you ever said to me. You don't remember, but I do. It was about your master's essay. You didn't know how you got in, etcetera. Of course, you ended up with the highest honors; but then, you always did. It's good to see you. You look as wonderful as ever."

"So do you. We both need, or soon will, reading glasses. One of the consolations of needing reading glasses is that without them everyone looks better. You look fine. Does Janet know you're here?"

"Of course she does. What's more she suspects me of having lured her into a bathtub for mysterious purposes. How was I to know Janet would be the woman of the century? I was simply asked to teach two writing courses, and I decided what the hell, I might as well see the East again. So I came. No one connected the name; the world is full of Mandelbaums. And here I am. And here you are, Fellow of the Institute and friend of Janet in the bathtub."

"Moon," Kate said, "if you mention a bathtub once more, I shall do, I know not what, but it shall be the terror of the earth. Dear Moon," she inconsequently added.

Moon Mandelbaum's given name was Milton, which he hated and never used. Milton Mandelbaum had become Moon before Kate met him. He was large, and poetic, and marvelous, and he had married Janet.

"Why did you marry Janet?" Kate asked.

"She was beautiful," Moon answered, knowing some questions had to be asked again and again, as they turned up in different contexts, "even more Gentile than you, if you know what I mean, and she wouldn't go to bed with me otherwise. Not, it turned out, because she valued her virginity, though women did much more in those days, but because she didn't much like going to bed. Janet isn't a very warm person, you know. She gets into twits. And, if you remember, *you* refused to marry anyone."

"Twits?"

"So and so insulted her. She doesn't like this man's manner, or that man's art. She's fool enough to like masterful men, and I was fool enough to play at mastery, and we ended up in church. To her parents' infinite regret, not to mention mine. Meanwhile, she became a famous scholar and I got tenure for running the writing program in Minneapolis. I hear you did marry, after all."

"Yes," Kate said. "Is it that long since I've seen you? He's in Africa, Asia, the Third World." Another world, she was thinking.

"As for me, I've been married twice since. No good. Perhaps it's me, but I rather think it's women. I don't want to be masterful; I don't want to be a success, I like sex a lot, and singing. I was glad to hear you were going to be here. Harvard is a lousy place, twenty-four carat, all through, lousy. You make it better."

Kate looked at Moon. He looked, after how many years? very much the same. Perhaps she needed glasses, but he did look the same. He still had an undefinable look of sweetness, he still had everything as far as she could see, including the same intense attractiveness. He had the effect on her that he had always had, had it still in her study off the Radcliffe Yard. Kate knew that she had experienced too much, too fast, and that she was going to give way. All that could save her was if Moon did not guess. But Moon had always guessed.

"All I have," he said, "is a lousy room almost at Central Square. Also a kitchen and bath. I've got a mattress on the floor, my guitar, a bottle of Tequila from a student who graduated last semester, male, he may learn to write, and a lemon. You busy?"

"Remember," the woman at the Institute who had shown Kate her study had said, "to lock it when you leave." Kate remembered.

Chapter 5

*Long afterward, Oedipus, old and blinded, walked
the roads.   He smelled a familiar smell.   It
was the Sphinx.   Oedipus said, "I want to ask one
question. Why didn't I recognize my mother?"
"You gave the wrong answer," said the Sphinx.
"But that was what made everything possible," said
Oedipus.   "No," she said. "When I asked, What
walks on four legs in the morning, two at noon, and
three in the evening, you answered, Man.   You
didn't say anything about woman." "When you say
Man," said Oedipus, "you include women too. Everyone knows that."   She said, "That's what you
think."*

MURIEL RUKEYSER
"Myth"

KATE'S LIFE AT HARVARD settled down to something
like a routine. Mornings she worked in her study at the
Institute; she agreed upon a date—near the end of the
semester—when she would give her public lecture
there. Gradually she came to know some of the other
Fellows, women who regarded her, as she did them, as
fortunate scholars having been given the gifts of time,
space and community.

When Kate was not working, she walked, always
around the Mount Auburn cemetery, sometimes alone,
sometimes with Moon or a woman friend. In Cambridge, there was nowhere else to walk. One of the dif-
ferences between Cambridge and New York, Kate was
amazed to discover, was that they did not clear snow

47

off the sidewalks in Cambridge. Yesterday's snow, melting, formed a layer of ice beneath tomorrow's snow. To walk fast, to walk on the sidewalks at all, was perilous. Kate who needed to walk each day, as she needed each day a certain space for solitude, had found the cemetery the answer. She soon learned to ignore the phallic monuments—and those flatter ones which declared, simply, "Mother"—and to praise the trees and lakes and birds. Spring, she was told, would bring the glory of the Japanese cherry and other flowering trees. Henry James and William Dean Howells, Kate learned, had walked here in their time, talking of the future of the American novel. One day, indeed, she crossed the street to the Cambridge cemetery to visit the grave of Henry James. She could never remember, in New York, visiting anyone's grave except, in her extreme youth, Grant's.

Once a month Kate was contracted to lunch at Dunster, with sherry beforehand in the Senior Common Room; these lunches were clearly destined to be gruesome occasions—this became clear after the first. The younger tutors at Dunster tended to band together; the few older men who were affiliated with the house—notable Fellows like Anthony Lewis of the *New York Times* rarely, if ever, Kate was told, turned up—were so stuffy, so unopen to any views but their own that, not for the first time, and certainly not only at Harvard, Kate despaired of the ability of the generations to communicate with each other. The younger faculty members either pandered to these older, snotty types, or avoided them. In either case, no exchange took place. Kate was thrown pretty continually in with the younger faculty, not only from preference, though it was her preference, but because as a woman, and a woman neither young nor luscious nor sycophantic, she was simply invisible to those who still viewed Harvard as an all-male institution.

Meanwhile, the mystery of Janet's evening at Warren House seemed no nearer to solution. Janet herself was not being a great success at getting to know people. She seemed half eager to talk with Kate, and they met from time to time, but without any progress in intimacy. What alone was clear was that Janet had come to Harvard with wholly unrealistic expectations. Although she could never bring herself to express to Kate exactly what her expectations had been, Kate could guess. At her former university, Janet had turned her back upon the whole idea of women; she had operated within her department, had been accepted, at least to her satisfaction, as one of the boys. Telling herself that any woman with qualifications could make it, she had been as strict as any man in judging the women who applied for jobs, or tenure. She had come to Harvard full of hope for the same scene, but better; that hope had been harshly denied.

Kate had just begun to conclude that her presence at Harvard was to be without any consequence whatever—the fate, of course, of all women at Harvard—when two pieces of good fortune overtook her. First, walking one morning up Brattle Street on her way to the Institute, Kate saw Jocasta. Cambridge dogs, as characteristic of Cambridge as all its other inhabitants, walked about with unusual insouciance and independence, whether accompanied or not. They crossed streets, ambled along sidewalks or, if so instructed, waited, untied, outside stores into whose interiors their human companions had disappeared. Thus Jocasta waited. At least, Kate was fairly sure it was Jocasta, but white bullterriers do resemble one another, and she paused alongside the dog awaiting recognition or scorn. Jocasta moved her snout slightly nearer to Kate's hand, and then licked it, perhaps remembering a comfortable couch and cold chicken covertly given in the kitchen. Kate knelt down and patted the dog; then she went into the store to look for Joan Theresa.

It was a flower shop which also sold beautiful pieces of fruit; by these Joan Theresa had been tempted. She, with Kate, emerged from the store eating an apple, and carrying a large grapefruit in her other hand ("Keep the bag and save our forests," she had told the storekeeper). Joan offered Kate a bite of the apple, as they joined Jocasta. Kate took a large bite.

"I'm sorry not to have yet got to the coffee shop," Kate said. "Somehow, once in Harvard, one forgets there are other parts of Cambridge. How is your friend who found Janet Mandelbaum in the bathtub?"

"Luellen May is terrible," Joan said. "Terrible. All the usual hassles, from her husband and all. About the kids, you know. Why don't you come one day soon and see what you can do? Cheer her up, maybe?"

"I'll come," Kate said. She bent down to nuzzle Jocasta. I'm batty about that dog, she thought.

The second occurrence was less expected. At the Institute in her second week there, Kate found a message: *Please call Professor Sladovski at this number.* Before calling this number, Kate looked Professor Sladovski up in the Harvard directory and discovered him to be an assistant professor in the English Department. Kate thought a moment before taking the plunge. It was, indeed, extraordinary, or would have been anywhere but Harvard, that no member of the English Department had made the slightest attempt to get in touch with her, nor had she discovered any avenues of approach to them. So Professor Sladovski might well be a breakthrough. (He might equally, Kate reminded herself, be an untenured professor in search of "contacts." All the better; she would use him as he hoped to use her.)

Professor Sladovski expressed delight at hearing from Kate; would she come to dinner, the professor ("Call me Andy") asked her; he and his wife, Lizzy, were eager to meet her. Kate considered dinner parties less trying than death by drowning, or six rounds on a roller coaster, but not much less. She had learned to say so.

"Oh, it's not a dinner party. Only me and Lizzy and Penny Artwright. Penny's an assistant professor in the department too. We thought you might be interested in chatting. Lizzy heard about you from her network; all reports were excellent."

"In that case, and hoping you will forgive my outspokenness, I'd love to come."

"Have you any special dietary requirements?"

"I eat anything but peanut butter and Coca-Cola. I'll bring some wine if I may."

"Lovely. Seven then." He gave her the address. "Also, we don't mind if you smoke."

"You *are* plugged into a network," Kate said.

"And about time too," Andy said, ringing off. Kate's spirits rose immoderately.

That afternoon Kate took a walk with Moon and, as it started to snow, went back with him to his room. "I'll play the guitar," he said. "We'll sit and sing and talk, and watch the snow."

Moon had played the guitar and sung when she met him in the fifties; he had begun long before that, long before the days of rock music. In fact, Moon always reminded Kate of Pete Seeger or, to be honest, the other way around, since she had first seen Pete Seeger in the seventies, during one rather frantic summer in the Berkshires. Actually, Kate recalled, she had begun by being annoyed with Pete Seeger, he seemed so out of the thirties, singing about how the banks owned all the farms, which may have been true once but certainly wasn't now. Then he had sung a song written, he said, by his sister, called "I'm Gonna Be an Engineer," and he had won her heart. She had since been to hear him sing once or twice, including a time at a New York college when he had sung songs in Yiddish in deference to his audience and had reminded Kate even more of Moon. Pete Seeger was fine, Kate had decided, except that his nose was too small. Every time he gestured toward the audience, encouraging them to sing, she thought of Moon, the same open, warm, welcoming gesture.

Moon was singing about a lady from Baltimore, and Kate thought how like this time was to the other times they had met. Always in cities that were not home to either of them, in rooms that were stopping places. Moon always traveled light. Sometimes he wrote marvelous letters, and sometimes she did not hear from him for years. She hoped that this tangle with Janet and

Harvard would not change their relationship—if it could be called a relationship—and take Moon from her life. Because Moon existed wholly apart from daily living; he ought never to marry anyone. Moon could meet you five, ten years later and pick up where he had left off, but she doubted if he was good on a daily basis. Even if Kate had meant, in youth, to marry, she would not have married Moon who was, after all, just waiting for the sixties to catch up with him and was even now not noticing especially that they had passed.

"Moon," Kate asked, when he put the guitar aside and joined her in a glass of wine, "is Harvard treating you well? Glad you came?"

"Not really glad, except for you. But the advantage of being a *visiting* teacher of writing is that you don't have to attend meetings, or get into department wrangles. Of course, stuffy meetings are meat and drink to your Janet; why not ask her?"

"She is not *my* Janet," Kate irritably said. "She used, may I tactlessly point out, to be yours."

"Do you know, I have trouble remembering I was married to her. She should have taken up with the sort of professor who would have had his first affair with another graduate student a year after they were married, and left her free to play the long-suffering wife. Instead, I made her *be* the long-suffering wife."

"By not sleeping with other graduate students?"

"By insisting on a real relationship. Real relationships make Janet nervous. I'll say this for Harvard: it's the only place, except possibly in New York, where I could have ended up teaching with Janet and never meet her or even remember that she's here. I'm sure she feels the same, or did until she thought I might have had a part in her unfortunate party."

"Moon, we must, I know, stop discussing Janet, which must be beastly for you . . ."

"I love it when you use words like beastly."

"But just tell me this: What do you think went wrong with Janet? Why is she in such a state? I don't just mean the party episode, even beyond that. She's like a cat on a hot plate, unable to find any place to put her feet down."

"That's just it. Janet got to the best place she could think of to be, and when she got there it had changed. Subtly, mysteriously, for all the wrong reasons, in her opinion, it had changed. Instead of being the queen, dining with her regiment, she had to take notice of other women; all her life Janet has ignored other women, even despised them. Frankly, I wouldn't be surprised if she resigned and asked for her old job back."

"Would they give it to her?" Kate asked. "Would it be the same if they did?"

"They'd probably give it back to her, if this little nastiness dies down. Nice to be preferred to Harvard. Janet would be a lot happier back where she came from, where she knew what was expected of her. People like Janet *can* go home again."

"I guess plenty of people wish she would," Kate said.

Andy and Lizzy Sladovski lived on the third floor of an ancient three-story house in a part of Cambridge near Harvard but not yet wholly encroached upon by that institution's unrelenting expansion. Kate no sooner arrived, and was seated around the table in their large living room, than she relaxed. Having bestowed her wine, she accepted a Scotch and put her feet up. Andy and Lizzy were likable in a way, it suddenly struck Kate, that so few people were these days: intelligent, not unduly tense, and wholly without pretense. Lizzy told Kate that she was a nurse who had been offered, only the other day, a position of importance administering a large section of a large hospital, but had declined the offer.

"Penny thinks you can't stay in one place," Lizzy said. "You either go forward or you stagnate. Penny believes there is a law of human nature which demands movement and resists stasis. Don't you, Penny?" Penny Artwright, unlike the Sladovskis, who were Catholic of Polish descent, was a WASP of the Fansler ilk, and like

Kate, had grown tired of her clan's self-satisfied view of life. Nonetheless, she dressed with great style, and had a certain nervous tension about her. Professors should have nervous tension, Kate thought, nurses not, so that was fine. What she noticed also was that Andy sat perfectly relaxed in the company of three women; nor did he comment on the situation.

"This doesn't seem much like Harvard," Kate said. "Not an original remark, but a comforting one. Comfort, now that I think of it, is rarely original. I've only had a sip of my drink, and already I'm sounding profound. Good atmosphere."

"Harvard makes one breathless," Penny said. "Everybody's always trying so hard. Last night I was summoned to the house of one of the senior professors, one of the few who bother with the underlings. He's very nice, really, but having dinner with him is a bit like being summoned to dine with the boss; exactly the same, now that I think of it. They invited an unattached male assistant professor along with me; you can't invite a *lone* woman; Harvard clings firmly to the Noah's Ark principle. Anyway, not only was the evening the last word in stilted conversation and dreary anecdotes, but my companion of the evening decided his way to the heart of the senior professor was to teach him and his wife bridge. Naturally, any Harvard professor who would have assistant professors to dinner is too kind, in a superficial way, to say he doesn't want to learn bridge, at least in so many words, but it was clear enough to me. Not to my thick-headed male companion. He had decided the way to promotion was to teach his elders and betters to play bridge, and that was that. A typical Harvard social occasion."

"Do you play bridge?" Kate asked.

"I do, but I denied it. That meant he couldn't call on me for any part in his silly campaign. I'll help a colleague out of a jam, but not out of lunacy. Besides, he doesn't approve of intellectual women, and probably thinks the female brain could only rise to the heights of bridge in service to a bridge-playing husband."

Kate chuckled. "My sister-in-law can never remember that I don't play bridge, and when they see me they always end up telling me about some finesse, if that's the word, they pulled off the other night. I do play poker, however, in the right company and at the right stakes."

"That of course," Andy said, "is the game everyone at Harvard plays for a living, with the wrong company and the wrong stakes. Shall we eat?"

They had dinner in the large, old-fashioned kitchen. There was a porch off it, lovely, the Sladovskis said, in the summertime. As they ate by candlelight, Kate realized that the comfort she felt was a unique experience for her at Harvard. It was not, of course, that she was ill at ease with Sylvia, or with Moon. But Sylvia had so much of the Washington air about her, so much the sense of strategies deployed, of time well used. And Moon, at the other extreme, was so at ease that Kate felt, perversely, drugged in his presence, overrelaxed. Only here, and for the first time since she had boarded the shuttle, did she feel simply herself.

Kate had just decided to be less comfortable and to bring up the subject of Janet Mandelbaum, when Lizzy did it for her. "We understand you were at graduate school with Andy's new queen bee," was how she introduced the subject.

"Indeed I was. In fact, we were the only two women in a male group all studying for their comprehensive examinations at the same time."

"And I bet our Janet got distinction."

"High distinction. And was beautiful into the bargain. Life seemed unfairly tilted in her direction in those days. It seems less so now."

"You're not going to start defending her!" Andy said.

"Sure I'm going to defend her," Kate said. "The women I don't defend are those who came along in the seventies sneering at the women's movement but reaping the rewards other women had won for them. Janet is a different matter altogether. None of you knows the price Janet paid for where she is. I don't think anyone can know except a woman who's been there. No more than other women was she preserved, as she achieved a reputation in the academic world, from the attacks of cruel and envious men. I wish to hell it hadn't been Janet they appointed; I wish one of those idiot men on the search committee had consulted a woman, if only for information about which kind of woman could stand the strain, but since they put her there, yes, I'm going to defend her."

"We heard you didn't like her," Penny said.

"Haven't I been telling you I don't like her? I can't like anyone incapable of intimacy—no, that's not true, I can't love anyone incapable of it. Janet is like a hedge-hog—all bristles the moment she might have to put someone's feelings above her own. I can't love her, then, and I can't like her because, poor dear, she isn't likable."

"Did they go out of their way to find someone no one could like?" Penny asked.

"I wouldn't put it past them," Andy said. "What gets me is that not even old Clarkville likes her; now I would have thought that she was just the sort to make that old pansy happy—always supposing one had to have a woman around at all. All right, I withdraw the word pansy," Andy said, looking at his wife. "It's just the way one uses any frightful epithet, racial, sexual, whatever, when one thoroughly dislikes a person and wants an easy way to say so. Clarkville's a weight who's going to sink that department if they don't throw him overboard. And who's going to throw Clarkville? He doesn't think they should have let women into Widener, he doesn't think we should have ended the Vietnam War, he thinks Nixon was railroaded, and he thinks labor unions should be outlawed. How did I get started on Clarkville?"

"He too dislikes Janet."

"Has he been beastly to you?" Kate asked Penny.

"No, not really; he's patronizing, vaguely flirtatious, and chivalrous. He knows I'm without power, and it makes him feel fair and noble to treat me with courtesy, even exaggerated courtesy. But he'd never support me for tenure, not here, not anywhere. He'll write that I'm very bright for so young and attractive a woman."

Penny tipped her chair back, and then brought it sharply forward. "I'll tell you what I *really* think about Clarkville, and all the others—about their intentions with the choice of Janet. Prepare to call me paranoid," she said to Lizzy, "but I bet you I'm right. Janet was chosen with great foresight; they couldn't refuse the endowment, but they made sure that they got someone, not only impeccable academically and all that, but also —are you ready?—someone they knew would crack."

"You're dreaming, my dear," Andy said. "Janet may be a bit bewildered at the moment, but I promise you she would have struck anyone who met her before she arrived at Harvard as the most solid person in the world. The *least* likely to crack."

"You give them too much credit, surely," Kate said to Penny, but she said it vaguely. Had they guessed that Janet had her circle of supporters, all male, of course, at her old university, and would be quite cut off here, exposed to the famous Harvard indifference and sangfroid?

"O.K.," Penny said, "I give them too much credit. I admit everyone I know who's been invited to Harvard and then ignored—from Junior Fellows to the most Senior Visiting Professors—always thinks there's a conspiracy to ignore them when it's just the wonderful Harvard manner. But if they didn't want her to crack, why did they dope her and drop her in a bathtub, and *then* call in the women most likely to make her look horrible in her own eyes?"

"Who," Kate asked, "is *they,* exactly?"

"Someone Clarkville put up to it, if you ask me," Andy said. "One of his acolytes at the party."

"In that case," Kate said, "he may not be satisfied with the results. Interest in the case is dying down, and perhaps because Sylvia and I are here, Janet is holding on. We provide an outlet. The bathtub bit didn't work."

"Kate, I wish they'd offered you the job," Penny said. Andy nodded in agreement.

"I'm flattered and pleased to hear it. But they didn't dare. They knew I wouldn't take it, but they weren't taking a chance. One real feminist in this place with tenure could cause—well, not damage, but trouble. Harvard and Yale and Princeton take a lot of care to see that they avoid trouble. The best way to avoid it is to be careful whom you have around, and in what numbers."

"Lots of people think they pick their students on that basis, among others," Andy said.

"You all amaze me," Lizzy said. "Whenever any of us get together, Harvard is all you talk about. Before Janet, it was other things: how badly the students are treated, how snotty the professors are, endless things. And yet, Andy and Penny both grabbed at the chance to come here. That's what Harvard lives on, that reputation. If some of the best of you, teachers and students, would say no and mean it, even Harvard might begin to guess it ought to change. But power can always buy what it wants. It even bought you in the end," she said to Kate.

"You mean the Institute. No, they didn't buy me. Nothing could have brought me here, really, except the Janet mess and a dreadful curiosity. I've always had a morbid fascination with institutions, the army, the church, the prestigious universities, they are so implacable. I can't take my eyes off them, as though they were a grotesque sideshow. And I want terribly to be present at the moment they begin to shake and change, if they ever do."

"So you came out of curiosity?"

"Curiosity, and being asked by friends and bullterriers." Kate smiled ruefully. "Most of all I came, if you want to know, because I'm bored. Whether because we've lost our audience for literature, or because one can't teach *Middlemarch,* not even *Middlemarch,* forever, or because I think the political movements, the social movements, are important now the way the humanities were important when I was beginning to teach—why did I begin this terrible sentence?"

"To say why you came to Harvard."

"Yes. I came because I think what happens here now, with Janet, matters; I don't think what happens in the English Department in my university matters bloody much, not at present. That's why I came."

Some days later, Kate was sitting in her study at the Institute, staring out at the Yard, which she did not see, constructing sentences. Kate molded sentences as a sculptor molds clay. The results vary, depending on the skill of the sculptor or the sentence molder, but Kate had always felt the process to be the same. The only sound was a typewriter in the next room. Nor was Kate's attention seriously diverted by a woman who came into the Yard and performed, in the snow, extraordinary exercises. She did this so regularly that she had become, for Kate, a part of the scenery, swaying like the trees. Kate was therefore startled by a knock on the door, not diffident, as knocks at the Institute tended to be, but imperative. Kate opened the door to find the receptionist, rigid with indignation. "We are *not* supposed to get calls for Fellows," she announced. "If they expect important calls, they are supposed to have a phone in their study. This person insisted, insisted that I get you, saying it was a matter of life and death. I hope it is."

Silent, worried and apologetic, Kate followed the young woman downstairs. She picked up the receiver with an ingratiating smile for the receptionist.

"Kate Fansler here," she said into the waiting phone.

"Professor Fansler? Clarkville speaking. English Department." ("I knew it," Kate said to herself, even then. "No woman could have convinced that receptionist it was important.")

"Yes?" Kate said. Was the English Department about to take some notice of her presence after all?

"I didn't know whom else to call, I'm afraid. Janet Mandelbaum had mentioned you. I've called the police, of course."

"The police?"

"She's dead, I'm afraid. Forgive me; this must be a shock, but . . ."

"Where is she?" Kate asked.

"She . . . I'm afraid she's in the men's room. That's where I found her."

"The men's room?"

"Here at Warren House. I thought I should let you know, let someone know. You'll probably be hearing from the police."

"Thank you for calling." Kate hung up the telephone and stared before her, so fixedly, that the receptionist asked her if something was the matter.

"The matter?" Kate said. And did not answer.

Chapter 6

Inconsistencies cannot both be right, but imputed to man they may both be true.
SAMUEL JOHNSON
Rasselas

" 'IN THE SPRING OF 1970,' I said to the policeman, 'there were no tenured women at Harvard. By the fall of 1970 there were two. I'm full of statistics like that,' I said to him, 'if they're any use to you.' "

"And what did he say?" Sylvia asked.

"He looked at me as though I were demented, of course, which turned out to be rather useful, since I managed to extract some facts from him."

"Without coming down too heavily on the fact that you are married to one of the leading authorities on police evidence, methods, etcetera?"

"Well, no, I did manage to suggest I was madly familiar with such matters; Reed, I rather implied, mumbles in his sleep about poisons, bodies moved after death, and so on. I expect that did help."

"Was the body moved after death?"

"Yes, thank God, it was. Thank God because one would have hated to explain what she was doing in the men's room. Thousands of reasonable explanations leap to mind, that is to your mind and mine, but we all know how the conventional mind works given half a chance."

"So someone moved her after she was dead and put her in the stall of the men's room."

"That's it."

"Why? I know, don't tell me. To discredit her. To

61

make her look metaphorically like someone who insisted on invading male territory. Poor Janet, who *loathed* that sort of woman. Life is unfair. And death. Did the policeman understand why you were rambling on about tenured women at Harvard?"

"Not really. They were more interested, naturally, in where the poison came from. Also in not upsetting Harvard, if possible. Say what you want about town and gown antagonisms, my impression was that on some upper levels, gown called the tune having paid the piper. Just a matter of influence, probably. I'm a suspect, of course. So is practically every member of the Harvard English Department, which is something of a comfort. So is Luellen May and the rest of the sisters, which is worrying. The policeman seemed fairly clear, naturally, that he was not expecting to arrest a Harvard professor of Clarkville's reputation, which makes it look even blacker for the sisters."

"He's probably right," Sylvia said. "Harvard has dealt with women effectively enough, without starting to kill them off now."

"Well, I don't know. It does seem as though this chair might have begun to look like the beginning of the end to the old Harvard establishment. The fact is, no one but the Harvard English Department, which didn't want and had never wanted a full-time, tenured woman member, had anything to gain from Janet's death. I know the police aren't that keen on motive, but I am. What else had anyone to gain?"

"Well, what about those women in the coffee shop on Hampshire?" Sylvia asked.

"What motive could they possibly have had? They wanted Janet calmed down, not bumped off."

"They seemed damn anxious about her, if you think a minute. Sending that woman, what was her name?"

"Joan Theresa."

"Yes, Joan Theresa, all the way to New York to entice you up here."

"And Jocasta."

"Who?"

"Never mind," Kate said. "I'm rambling. The fact is, as I hope you realize, I don't know a thing about the Harvard English Department. Short of getting hold of a catalog, I don't even know the names of the members. My position here seemed strangely anomalous, when I tried to explain it. The poor policeman couldn't quite figure out where I came in, as a matter of fact, or why Clarkville had called me first when he found the body."

"It certainly is a mark of poor Janet's condition here that there was no one else to call," Sylvia said. "Of course, there was Moon."

"Clarkville could scarcely have known about Moon. You only know because I told you. I'm sure Janet didn't tell anyone, and certainly Moon didn't."

"I wonder what Moon's ideas are."

"No doubt," Kate said, "I shall learn before long. Sylvia?"

There was a pause while Sylvia looked up questioningly. There lay between them the sense of things unsaid, but not, as so often with good friends, of things unsaid but understood. They were adrift, they did not know what questions they wanted to ask, nor even in what sense, apart from the terrors and pity of any death, they should mourn Janet. "The fact is," Kate said, "women, at least around here, live in a never-never land, not certain where they belong, where their allegiances lie, not even what their hopes are. It's no different in New York, of course, except that New York itself consists in not belonging, at least for a great many people in it."

"You mean you're sad about poor Janet, who had the best of all the women bargains, it would appear, and you're angry with Joan Didion."

"Joan Didion. The writer?"

"I just read in *Time* magazine," Sylvia said, "that Joan Didion dismisses the women's movement 'with some hauteur.' Wait a minute, I've got it right here, her own lovely words. 'To those of us who remain committed mainly to the exploration of moral distinctions and ambiguities, the feminist analysis may have seemed a parti-

cularly narrow and cracked determinism.' That's what
Didion says. *Time* says she has contempt for the wom-
en's movement as cant. She admires Georgia O'Keeffe.
Who the hell doesn't admire Georgia O'Keeffe? Why am
I so angry at Joan Didion, for God's sake? She writes
good novels, even if she does write them in Hollywood.
And don't ask me what all this has to do with Janet, I
don't know."

"Nothing seemed to have anything to do with Janet.
That was her problem. She wasn't in Hollywood dealing
with moral distinctions, she was at Harvard. And she
wouldn't, or couldn't, admit that the only possible support would have to come from women."

"Joan Theresa knows *that*."

"Ah, but Joan Theresa has crossed another important line. She has moved away from men altogether,
and from women who live with men. What's more, she
doesn't think male institutions, Harvard or any other,
are worth belonging to. Rotten places using rotten pro-
cesses, to which we prostitute ourselves, you and me.
We're in the smallest class, Sylvia, just a few of us hud-
dled here."

"Like an unmarried Victorian daughter who's had a
baby, thrown out into the storm."

"Or if not thrown out, made to suffer, filled with re-
morse. What we need," Kate said, "is a drink."

Kate was considerably more worried about Luellen
May and the Maybe Next Time Coffee House than she
cared to admit to Sylvia or even to herself. For one
thing, she thought it likely that the police would hit on
Luellen May, if not gladly, at least with relief, as the
likeliest suspect. For another thing, and Kate, riding the
subway to Central Square, admitted this to herself reluctantly, Luellen May seemed to her, Kate the great
detective, a likely suspect. Why? Was she, with her
scorn for Harvard, nonetheless unable to believe them
capable of murdering Janet? Was she readier to suspect
a woman disaffected by the Harvard community than
the Harvard community itself? Uncomfortable as such

thoughts were, Kate faced them, as was her wont, and realized that if she had them, the police would have them twice as vehemently.

Kate was on her way to the coffee house in order to clear her mind. No doubt part of the problem came from unfamiliarity with the world of Joan Theresa and Luellen May. Kate was, moreover, annoyed with herself for not having looked the sisters up earlier, before Janet had been killed and ordinary relationships rendered impossible, or at least unlikely. Still, she consoled herself, she had been at Harvard only a few weeks; it was only early February, even if, considering one thing and another, Kate felt she had been at Harvard for years.

The Maybe Next Time Coffee House turned out to be on the ground floor of a characteristically large Cambridge house, too far out to interest Harvard. The kitchen, in the back part of the room, was open, and Kate could see two women working there, one of them kneading bread. It looked very wholesome, brownish, made with whole-wheat, or unbleached flour, or whatever. Kate was aware of eyes turned toward her, and away: the point of such a coffee house was that a woman could enter alone and not feel conspicuous, or likely to be hassled. She sat down at a table, wondering if she should fetch the food herself from the counter, but presently a woman appeared to ask her what she wanted. Kate ordered capuccino and some sort of sandwich, and asked for Joan Theresa.

"Tell her it's Kate," Kate said, falling back on the new first name culture. "I've come to see how Jocasta is, and about a few other things. She did invite me."

"That's fine," the young woman said, reassuringly. "My name is Betty. I think she's upstairs."

Kate's sandwich, when it arrived, seemed to be an open piece of whole-wheat bread which Kate, despising, felt guilty about despising, on which was an assortment of vegetables, including the inevitable bean sprouts. Kate sipped her coffee and tried to decide why she did not feel comfortable. Nothing could have been more reassuring than this humble restaurant, with the cooks in the back and notices all over the wall—rock concerts, discussion groups, apartments needed. No, the problem wasn't entering an unknown world, it was that, being here, one defined oneself too sharply: either one was an observer from the outside, automatically "other," or else one qualified to be a member of the club, which limited one in a different way. Was this how a Leftist felt in England in the thirties, attending the first Socialist meeting? Hard to stay away, impossible to join?

Kate was aroused from these ruminations by the arrival of Joan Theresa and another woman. "Well," Joan Theresa said, "quite a surprise, seeing you here. The immediate result, no doubt, of their bumping off that poor woman up at Harvard. This is Luellen May, the woman I mentioned who was called to Warren House."

Kate shook hands. "How is the custody case going?" she asked.

"God knows. My ex-husband, known to all his friends as the monster, doesn't want the children, he just wants to keep me from having them. Since he's trying to prove I'm unfit, my getting involved in a drunken brawl didn't help." Luellen May looked to Kate exactly like the sort of woman to whom she would have awarded custody of children, any children, on the spot. Kate thought how Luellen's words, read out in court, could sound mean and vengeful, but that, expressed in Luellen's gentle voice, they seemed only to state a fact. Trying to decide whom Luellen reminded her of, she traced a flimsy memory back to her mother's distant admiration for a film actress, Madeleine something, Madeleine Carroll, than whom no one could have looked less murderous. I am going bonkers, Kate thought, my mind is becoming disorderly, like Reed's top bureau drawer. She poked a bit at her bean sprouts.

"The thought is," Kate finally said, "that some women think all men are monsters. Saying so in court, therefore, is likely to be seen in the wrong way."

"You seem to understand, at least a little," Joan Theresa said.

"What I don't understand," Kate said, "is who called you to Warren House? How did it happen?"

"You mean in the first place?" Luellen asked. "Of course, now the poor woman's been murdered, the police suspect me of having something to do with that. They questioned me. Hadn't I been part of marches where people were arrested? Didn't I run an all-women's coffee shop that was pretty antagonistic to ordinary people with their families and responsibilities? I know I can't make you see the sneer behind all this, the absolute belief that people like me are the ones who do such things. It's not the way they questioned you, I'm sure. They just kept beating away at me, *knowing* I'm guilty, hoping to make me say or do something that will let them prove it." Her voice broke. "One of the things I guess we won't agree about is the police," she said more softly, crying now.

"Let's stick to the point," Joan Theresa said.

"Isn't it the point?" Luellen asked. "Sorry," she added, rubbing her eyes. "I'm just so worried about my kids. All right, we'll take one thing at a time. The bathtub bit at Warren House. God knows how that happened; I barely managed to remember where Warren House is."

"Haven't you any connection with Harvard?" Kate asked.

"Oh, yes, I went there for a year. Then I dropped out. To go to Harvard from Boise, Idaho, that was supposed to have been the absolute end of life; to have made it. My family hasn't forgiven me yet for throwing over what they had always wanted for me, just as it was in my hands. The trouble was, you see, I succeeded too well; if I hadn't made it quite to Harvard, I might still have thought there was a chance for me in the system. But Harvard—the oxygen was too pure. I knew I couldn't survive it, and I seemed unable even to tolerate the company of those who liked that unreal life. Unreal was what it seemed to me, tired as that phrase is, and it still does. What I've learned since, I grant you, is that insofar as reality means no money, no ties to the system, no power, you can sure have too much of it."

Discussions of reality always made Kate long for a cigarette. The no-smoking signs in this place were palpable.

"And I fell," Luellen continued, "into the woman's inevitable trap. I married and worked at some dead-end job to support my husband and myself. After a while, when he'd gone back to law school, and the kids came, I was still working to support us, and doing all the housework—the same old dreary story. I found out he was sleeping with a fellow student. She'd come to the house, talk to me, help with the kids, and yet she did that. So I was through, you see, with women and men and the lot. I went on welfare. You didn't want to hear the story of my life, you wanted to hear how I ended up at Warren House. It hasn't much to do with all this."

"I'm sure it does," Kate said. "Go on."

"That's all. Except that when I didn't see how I was going to make it alone, I discovered there were other women in the same situation. We bought this house here, we share expenses and child care. Some of them run this coffee house. For the first time I had a community, and people who really wanted to share my life and my children's lives, and whose lives I could share."

"Are you still working at dead-end jobs?"

"No. I turned out to be rather smart with computers, and I trained as a programmer. The women here staked me while I went through the training, and now I have a good job and I'm paying back. But my husband says his children aren't going to grow up in a house full of women. I'm sure you can guess what he says. Not that he cares at all for the children. Which is why the custody trial is such a problem. And now this."

Kate smiled at Luellen. "I'm afraid I still don't see how you got to Warren House. I'm glad to know how you got here."

"I was coming to that, believe it or not. One of the guys who had a room in the same house as mine in the Yard freshman year went on to graduate work in English; I've seen him around, we talk when we meet. He didn't call that night, actually, it was one of his friends, anyway, another student whom I'd met. This guy said, 'One of your housemates is sloshed in the bathtub here. If you don't want a royal stink, you'd better come and get her out.' Well, like a fool, I just ran off without even checking. It didn't occur to me it was a hoax. When I got there, it was that Janet Mandelbaum. We were both pretty horrified, needless to say."

"Luellen's problem," Joan Theresa said, "is that despite a hard life, she has never really taken account of the perfidy of life."

"Did you know it was Janet Mandelbaum then?"

"No, I didn't. I learned that later. I did get her out of the bathtub before the cops came; everyone else had split by then, of course. A brave lot."

"Even your friend, the guy from the Yard?"

"I never saw him at all. Of course, I wonder now if he was ever there."

"Why didn't you ask him?" Kate asked.

"I wanted to keep as far away as possible. I wondered if he hadn't been put up to the whole thing by my husband. It would have been a clever plot, discrediting Janet and me in one swoop. But I thought, the less fuss I made, the less trouble."

"What women have always thought," Joan Theresa said.

"Certainly what poor Janet thought," Kate admitted. "Would you give me the name of the man who called you? And of the friend who lived near you freshman year?"

"Why not? If Joan here is willing to trust you, I am." Kate pushed a notebook across the table, and Luellen wrote the names down. "The top one's my friend," she said. "I've written that next to his name. The other man's also a graduate student in the English Department, the one who called me."

"Have the police asked about any of this?"

"No." Kate saw the two women exchange glances. "We didn't tell the police I'd been called. They didn't seem to know. They just knew I'd been there when she was found; all sort of routine. I decided not to enlighten them."

"You don't think it might be better to tell the truth; the whole story?"

Joan Theresa looked at Luellen as though to say: I'll handle this one. "Look, Kate, I know that you believe in a world with honest policemen. I don't want to say there aren't honest policemen, but most of the people I know don't meet up with them. It's no use getting all anecdotal, is it? It just seems to us that, for people without power, the police couldn't care less."

Kate was silent. She did not doubt the truth of what was said; she had heard enough from Reed, and knew through Reed a young policeman who had left the force in New York because if you did not condone police dishonesty, you could not remain on the force. Nor was she naïve: one does not deal on faculty committees for long and continue to believe in truth as an ideal widely practiced. People believe what it is convenient for them to believe. For me, however, Kate thought, it is convenient to believe in the police. "I saw too many movies when I was young in which good triumphed," she said. "I know that. But since I haven't separated myself wholly from institutions, I have to believe to some extent in their power to operate fairly. I have a feeling, however, that this isn't a discussion likely to lead to a useful conclusion. To be practical: if the police find out you were called, and you didn't mention it, won't that look bad?"

"Probably. If they decide to go after me, everything will look bad."

"Not exactly. There are still courts of law. And your having to say you lied when questioned by the police."

"I didn't lie. I just didn't offer information. Besides, you're supposed to be a great detective; you clear me. You have all the right contacts, the right friends, or did I get it wrong? Isn't that the way it goes?" she asked, looking at Joan Theresa. "Or aren't we the sort you pull strings for?"

Kate was sharply aware that Luellen, close to tears, did not appeal to her as Joan Theresa did. All unaccountable, and who you like, Kate my girl, she said to herself, has nothing to do with it. "Suppose it wasn't your ex-husband trying to discredit you. Why else do you think someone would have called?"

"I thought that would be pretty clear," Joan Theresa said, just not adding: even to a smart-assed professor of English literature! "To discredit Janet. To make people think she was involved with women like us."

"It seems a rather long shot."

"Not really. Someone called the campus police," Luellen said, "and they found out who I was. They said, 'What are you two doing here together?' Janet almost died of shame."

Joan Theresa said to Kate, "Why not come out with me and I'll get Jocasta. I'll walk with you." It seemed to be clear to Luellen that she was not to join them.

While Kate paid, Joan Theresa went upstairs for Jocasta. Woman and dog were waiting outside for Kate. "Shall we walk toward Harvard Square?" Joan said. "Jocasta will be forever in your debt, won't you, Jocasta?" The dog greeted Kate perfunctorily; her mind was on the possibility of an excursion. When she saw that they were actually going to go, she gave a little leap forward, setting off in a businesslike manner to follow scents and enjoy herself.

"Did you walk her all the way to Harvard Square the day I saw her outside a store?" Kate asked.

"No. We have a car here we use between us. Luellen took it the night she went over to the rescue of a sister, as she thought. Jocasta, you bitch, if you bother that Yorkie, I'll clobber you." Kate watched the hair in a ridge all down Jocasta's back settle down after Joan had grabbed her collar and thrust her on.

"I wanted to ask you something for Luellen, actually," Joan said.

"Not before I ask you something," Kate answered. "You came all the way down to New York to get me.

You said Janet wanted me. How did you know Janet wanted me, and why did you care if she did?"

"What I told you was the truth."

"But how could Luellen or you know that Janet knew me, let alone care if I came up to Harvard and calmed her down. In fact, I wouldn't have done so except for a call from another quarter. The whole thing doesn't make much sense."

By this time they had reached the part of Hampshire Street near Elm, not a part of Cambridge with which the parents of Harvard students are acquainted. It was what a social worker would call an interstitial neighborhood, running mostly to garages and light industry, with houses interspersed. And that's how you could describe me, Kate thought ruefully: an interstitial person.

"Here's the whole of it," Joan said. "The campus cops came and found the two of them, and they didn't believe Janet was a professor, of course, but they didn't want to act as though she were God knew what till they found out for sure, so they took the two of them to their headquarters, whatever they're called, and there were a lot of calls, and Janet dried off, and I guess it must have come over her that what she had said to Luellen was pretty God-awful. Janet was sorry I guess, and said what a mess everything was for her too—I don't know the details, but she mentioned you. She seemed to have you in her head as a woman who could cope. Well, Luellen got it into *her* head that maybe you would bring Janet round in some way, and that maybe you or Janet would help Luellen with her children."

"Help her?"

"Well, frankly, I think it's a little far out, but it seemed worth a trip to New York, particularly since someone was driving, and my brother lives there. I like to see him once a year. You see, Luellen's husband doesn't want the kids, he hasn't seen them in years, but he's out to stop her having them, and a lot of people are willing to help him, particularly if they've been born again. But if someone like you or Janet would testify for her . . . well, propriety, it would maybe do it. Her lawyer told her that. But it had to be some really straight people, with clout, who would go into court and say Luellen is the steadiest thing. Which she is. But of course, when the case comes up, she'll go in drag."

"Drag?" Kate said. They had stopped walking, and Jocasta was squatting at Joan's feet. Kate stared at Jocasta as though she might be a sister dressed as a bull-terrier. Could there have been something in the coffee? "Drag?" she repeated.

"Sorry about that," Joan said. "It's the word we use for dressing like, like . . ."

"I get it. Like me. A judge would take my word about whom to give children to because of the way I dress."

"It would help. We have a few of those outfits around the house, for getting drivers' licenses, things like that. Sorry, I wasn't trying to be offensive. Anyway, I didn't mean anything as elegant as you. You know, dresses with pearls and handbag."

"Spare me the details," Kate said. "You've just finished telling me, and you told me even more clearly in New York, that you'll use men and women who work with men any way you can to get what you want. Why should I let you use me?"

"A good question," Joan said. Kate, watching her, realized that Joan was afraid for Luellen, and not alone for Luellen's children. She was afraid that Luellen, feeling trapped and resentful, had in fact killed Janet in the men's room at Warren House, saying: stay there, where you always wanted to be! Luellen might need help badly, and Joan Theresa was preparing the way.

Joan, perhaps guessing at Kate's thoughts, went on the offensive. Or were these women that way anyhow, by nature, or by training? "You know," Joan said, "they may even think you killed Janet. Have you got an alibi?"

"I don't know," Kate said. "They don't know exactly when or where she died."

"Didn't she die in the men's room at Warren House?"

"No. She was moved there, some time afterward."

"What did she die of? The papers didn't say."

"Cyanide," Kate said. "Very fast and very nasty. If there's anything you can do, I'll be in touch. But I won't promise to swear Luellen is a fine type unless I think she is. I'm still that straight, and probably always will be."

"That," Joan said, "doesn't worry me. Luellen's a born mother, and a damn good person besides. She's just upset; you'll see."

The three of them turned down Cambridge Street.

"Cyanide," Sylvia said to Kate later that night. "I ask you, where did it come from?" Sylvia, her feet up, contemplated the view. When she had first seen her apartment, and later when Kate had seen it, they had supposed they would spend leisurely evenings having a drink on the balcony which ran the entire length of the living room, beyond the French windows. Alas, all such ideas are these days more tantalizing in prospect than in fact. The waves of carbon monoxide from the highway running below were suffocating; the noise was deafening; the dirt was fierce. Sylvia and Kate had, upon Kate's arrival, retreated indoors, where they now watched the passing February scene through glass.

"What we've got to do," Kate said, "is find out where the cyanide came from. And lots of other facts too, while we're at it. Damn it, Sylvia, let's pull what strings we can, yours reaching to Washington or the higher reaches of Harvard diplomacy, mine reaching to Wompompouchi, or wherever Reed is. All these types you know will do you a favor if you ask, won't they?"

"How nice to see Kate Fansler, the great detective, at work at last. Getting her friends to pull strings; I might have known that was how it worked. Of course there are all sorts of important young men, and some not so young, who will do things for me. Men can no longer be sure that women won't be useful to them one day in the hard, workaday world. Nancy Mitford used to claim that one had always to be nice to young girls, because one never knew whom they would marry. We've varied that a little, praise be."

"Glad to hear it. Let's get someone to persuade the police here, ever so quietly if they like, and with whatever excuse they like, to let us know what they know so far. Considering your connections with both Washington and Harvard, why don't you begin? If you strike out, I'll try Reed. But if you strike out, it will be madly significant."

"Madly. I see what you mean."

"If there are forces at Harvard who need to prevent your seeing this routine material, that will tell us more than the report will."

"Clever girl. I shall telephone tomorrow. In fact, I shall telephone now. George, by the way, is coming tomorrow; did I forget to tell you in the midst of all this?"

"So you did, damn it. Back to my tiny suite in Dunster. I'm told I should be madly grateful to have got it at all; you must really have thrown your weight around there. What I hate most is the food. Well, back to the dining room and student conversation. Speaking of which, I think I'll invite Leighton over. I've grown rather fond of Leighton."

"By which, of course, you mean that she's going through a rigorously anti-Fansler phase. I hope it lasts."

"It will. Leighton is full of promise. Are you glad George is coming?"

"Damn glad," Sylvia said. "I don't know why togetherness was ever held up as an ideal of marriage. Away from home for both, then together, that's much *better*. I'll send any police reports over to Dunster, to take your mind off the food."

Chapter 7

I should hate to live with a literary aunt.
STEVIE SMITH
Novel on Yellow Paper

NEXT DAY, from her room in Dunster, Kate called Andy Sladovski to discover, if possible, what state the English Department was in.

"Who knows?" Andy said. "If you want a shot at finding out, why not come with me tonight to the Harvard Iambics. They read papers on poets. You can't claim to have visited Harvard till you've been there."

"But no one's asked me."

"I'm asking you. Some extravagantly dull student, one of Clarkville's pets, is delivering a paper on Browning's 'Fra Lippo Lippi.' I can promise you the effort not to yawn will be excruciating, but there'll be food and drinks afterward, and you can sort of sniff around. You are, aren't you, interested in Browning? Your period, I seem to remember."

"I've all the proper credentials, except not having been asked."

"We only ask prominent visitors. Actually, one of the men brings his wife, so I could bring Lizzy, I suppose, but Lizzy wouldn't come unless they were discussing *The Golden Notebook,* which is unlikely for at least three overpowering reasons, only one of which has to do with metrics. Maybe they'll think you're Lizzy."

"Stop," Kate said. "I accept. Does it matter if I tend to look at Browning in a rather unscholarly manner?"

"Sounds refreshing. We're meeting at Adams House. Do you know where it is?"

"I know where a map is. Why Adams House?"

"That's where Howard Falkland is a tutor. Whoever reads the paper plays the host."

"Now there," Kate said, hearing the name of the paper reader with a start, "is a good idea. What attention you lose with your analysis, you can recapture with the food."

"Eight o'clock," Andy said, ringing off. Well, Kate said to herself, Fra Lippo Lippi: "God uses us to help each other so,/Lending our minds out." Browning was thinking about art, but I'm thinking about murder.

At five of eight, Kate stepped into the SCR at Adams House, and settled herself in one of the leather chairs arranged in a circle. Portraits of Harvard worthies, Kate assumed, glowered from the walls. By the time Andy had joined her, it was clear that they were not more than eleven in number, of whom one other was a woman: the wife, presumably. "We shall begin," Clarkville entoned. Kate had been amused to discover that he had not recognized her. One middle-aged woman looked remarkably like another to Clarkville. "We meet tonight," he continued, "to hear a paper by Howard Falkland on Browning. After the paper we will have questions. After the questions, we'll have the usual refreshments. We disband at ten. Howard."

Kate was never to remember what Howard Falkland said on the subject of Browning; indeed, she was not certain that she followed more than ten words at a time. The best of papers, read aloud, is hard to follow. This was not the best. But Kate had amusement enough. She found she could not take her eyes off Clarkville; he fascinated her, horrified and attracted her simultaneously, like a rabbit with a snake. There was no way in which Clarkville could sense her fascination, since his entire posture was designed to elude anyone's catching his attention or reading anything other than a certain drowsiness on his countenance. Clarkville was seated on a large leather couch, seated in the sense that his buttocks

and the couch had, at some climactic moment, encoun-
tered each other. From there Clarkville, a large and un-
gainly man, had slumped backward, so that he was as
close to reclining as one can be on a couch without actually stretching out on it; his eyes were directed ceil-
ingward and were shut. But he was not asleep; no, he
was listening. This was testified to by his pocket watch
which he had removed from his vest and now dangled
by its long chain, from one raised hand so that the
round gold watch moved back and forth with an agonizing regularity. It was extraordinary how annoying
this minor motion was, and how hard it was to keep
one's eyes off it. Kate did not try; Howard Falkland,
reading his paper, did not need to. Everyone else stared
alternately at Howard, the floor, the ceiling. Kate's eyes
sought Andy's, and he winked. Howard's voice droned
on. And this, Kate said to herself, is the highest reaches
of American academia. What she thought about was
not Browning or Fra Lippo Lippi, who would have
found this occasion even sillier than she did, but the
man who was the friend of the friend of Luellen's. *His*
name, of course, was Howard Falkland. Browning
scholarship certainly seemed doomed if its future prac-
titioners were qualified to be the subject of one of the
dramatic monologues.

When the reading was at last, mercifully, not a moment too soon, over, there were murmurings of appreciation and interest. Very gently, they all edged their
way toward the food—which was, indeed, an impressive spread.

"Did you prepare all this food yourself?" Kate asked,
when Andy had introduced her to Howard. Had Reed
been there, he would have recognized that Kate had
gone into one of her "ladylike" phases, always a dangerous sign.

"Not I," said Howard. "A woman I know did it for
me."

"Of course," Kate said. "I am *so* entranced by all
Harvard customs. I'm a guest of Andy Sladovski's, by

the way." Kate was rewarded by seeing Howard edge away from her: definitely *not* worth knowing.

"Well," Andy asked, "did Howard demand your credentials?"

"Didn't have a chance," Kate said. "I passed myself off as a maiden aunt, yours I think. For years," Kate added, inconsequentially, "I was a maiden aunt. Quite a nice role, really. Interesting and not exhausting."

"Good luck this time; here comes Clarkville. Let's see whether he accepts you as a maiden aunt, or decides you're my wife. He's only met Lizzy five times."

But greatly to Kate's disappointment, Clarkville had now remembered who she was. He had determined upon cordiality.

"Are you interested in Browning?" Clarkville asked.

"I'm a professor of Victorian literature," Kate mildly answered.

"Oh, yes," he said, "some university in New York."

"That's right," Kate said. "One or the other."

"Had I known," Clarkville said, "I would have asked you to join our group. The Harvard Iambics, you know."

"That would have been very kind of you," Kate said. How long, she asked herself, can I keep this up? Andy had melted away.

"The police don't seem very happy about our, er, little occurrence last week," Clarkville confided.

"No? Have they been to see you?"

"Oh, well, only to take a statement after I'd, er, found her. Poor woman; poor, poor woman. So out of her depth."

In the men's room or the department, Kate madly wanted to ask. "Out of her depth?" she merely echoed, feeling exactly like a character in a James novel.

"Well, you know, coming to Harvard, this department, strange city; the whole idea was ill-advised, ill-advised." He might have muttered thus forever, had Kate not excused herself to get a drink, which she felt she had well earned.

Walking home later with Andy, Kate admitted herself intrigued that Clarkville had never heard of her. "Great fame in the critical world I do not claim," she said; "still, I have, or thought I had, what my male colleagues call a national reputation. They have heard of me, if not in Peoria or Pocatello, Idaho, at least in most places that can boast even a minor branch of a major university. I'll bet Clarkville has heard of many men of less reputation."

"My dear Kate," Andy said, "if you haven't come from Harvard, what on earth would be the point of having heard of you? Besides, who hears of women till one is forced to hire them? What can you be thinking of?"

"What, indeed?" Kate said.

Leighton was glad enough, the next evening, to sup with her aunt in the dining hall at Dunster. They were joined by a group of Leighton's friends. The conversation, not surprisingly, centered on how absolutely, indescribably horrible Harvard was, not because a woman had been murdered here, but because it was, inevitably, horrid.

"But why," Kate asked, not for the first time and not, she suspected, for the last, "did you come here? I understand Leighton's reasons: she wanted a place where no one would pay the slightest attention to her. But you can't all have been hoping simply to be ignored."

The answers varied: Cambridge, and its delights. The proximity to Boston with all its other cultural amenities. The name. To be able to say one had gone to Harvard. The conviction that one does not turn down Harvard. Because it is there, like Mount Everest. Because one would certainly find, in so large a place, someone who shared one's interests.

"And have you?" Kate asked, picking up this last point. She directed her question pleasantly at a rather quiet, almost sullen girl sitting across the table. She had something of Janet's expression, Kate thought.

"No," the girl said, "I haven't. I know it's my fault,

the others tell me it is, but everyone I meet here seems so, well, superficial, interested either in marks, or in sex, or in having an intense relationship which is always so conventional they might as well have read about it in a book—or, well, frankly, dull, and self-absorbed. I know," she went on, "you're thinking, aren't I self-absorbed, and of course I am. But I do think I'm capable of being interested in someone else who doesn't look cool, or smooth, or as though she could pose for the centerfold in *Playboy*."

Kate refused to be diverted by *Playboy*. "But that's the oldest complaint about college everywhere. If one isn't cut to that year's pattern, one is lonely and excluded, unless one is very smart, very rich, or very secure. What makes Harvard different?"

"Almost no one is happy here," one of the boys offered.

" 'Happiness goes like the wind, but what is interesting stays.' Georgia O'Keeffe said that. And," she added, remembering Sylvia reading from *Time*, "everyone admires Georgia O'Keeffe, even Joan Didion."

"I *told* you she keeps quoting," Leighton said triumphantly. "But you haven't been doing it much lately," she added to Kate. "Leo says you've changed."

"Nephews and nieces always think one's changed because they have themselves grown up. However, I do quote less. There don't seem to be so many applicable quotes anymore, at least not in the authors I read in my establishment education. But now that I think of it," Kate said, "there is one." She glanced wickedly at Leighton.

"Oh, go on," Leighton said, with assumed weariness. "I've warned them."

"Well, Strether, in *The Ambassadors*, said of some other characters what I might say of you. 'You're my youth, since somehow at the right time nothing else ever was.' Janet Mandelbaum, however," Kate went on, firmly returning to her task, "would not have agreed. Did any of you know her?"

"I did," one young man answered. (I must stop

thinking of them as boys and girls, Kate thought.) "I'm interested in Simone Weil, and therefore in Herbert. She was quite helpful, though of course she did bristle a bit if one suggested that Herbert was a contemporary. Still, she explained his religion in a way which made Weil clearer. I was grateful."

"What was her manner like?" Kate asked.

"Professional. Not at all personal, as some of the younger profs are. She didn't call me by my first name, and I would never for a moment have thought of calling her by hers, ever. Oh, that's superficial, I know. But with all her dignity and distance, I thought she was always glad to see me."

"Did you know why?"

"Yes," the boy said, indicating, Kate thought, that it still took brains to get into Harvard and that brains still wanted to go there, "I didn't present any of the problems the women students did: I wasn't asking her for support as a woman. Also, I wasn't trying to be with it, I'm really interested in the seventeenth century, even if only as an adjunct to Weil. I'm in religion, which she liked. And I treated her as though . . ." The young man stopped.

"As though she were a man, a male professor." Kate said it for him.

"Yes," he said. "That's what she was like, I think. She didn't like to think of herself primarily as a woman. Of course," he added, "I don't mean . . ."

"I know exactly what you mean. She didn't think of herself as a man sexually, physically, psychically: that's Freudian nonsense. But she thought of herself as a full-fledged member of the brotherhood of professors, males all. Of course she did. And you know," Kate sadly added, "I think she died for that."

"Judith here met her too," Leighton offered, to rescue them from the silence that followed. "I dragged her here by the hair so you could talk to her. Judith loses all her nerve when she isn't being a reporter."

"I work for the *Independent*," Judith said. *"Much* better than the *Crimson,"* she added, as though countering a thought of Kate's of which Kate was wonderfully innocent.

"A newspaper," Kate rather foolishly said.

"Yes. Which doesn't think of itself as snootily, well, Harvard, if you know what I mean."

"I must read it," Kate said. "It's rather hard to get on to everything so fast. All I seem to see is the *Gazette*."

"That just tells you what's going on next week," Judith said. "Anyway, they sent me over to interview her because she was the new woman professor, you know, all that, and anyway when I asked her, she said she didn't want to talk about that, on the phone you know, so I said well I just wanted to know how she liked Cambridge, which was crap, but I had to get to her and she, well, you know, she delivered a long lecture on how women would never get anywhere if they kept interviewing each other as women. What I should ask her about, she said, was her professional work."

"And did you?"

"Well, my field is not English, so I didn't know much about the seventeenth century. But Leighton here is a nut on *Tristram Shandy*."

"The eighteenth century," Kate could not stop herself from saying.

"Well, close. So I asked Leighton about *Tristram Shandy*. But all I could remember was that the father screwed after winding a clock, and that Tristram had his dick cut off in a window, I didn't honestly think that . . ."

"Not his dick," Leighton sternly said with, Kate noticed, perfect seriousness, "he was circumcised. If you get everything wrong, how can you be a reporter?"

"I'd say that was the main qualification," Kate said. "Did Professor Mandelbaum want to talk about *Tristram Shandy?*"

"Oh," Judith said, "she rambled on about Locke for a while. We got exactly nowhere. Read my books, she said. Well, I ask you, for this we formed a committee and fought for the rights of women at Harvard? For this we started the *Seventh Sister?* Another newspaper," she added, seeing Kate's questioning look. "Read her books! I could read anyone's books, if I was interested in their boring subject. That's not an interview."

"I see," Kate said.

"I thought," Judith went on, "maybe I could interview you."

"But I'm just a Fellow at the Institute," Kate said.

"Typical female depreciation," Judith observed. "Just."

"You shall interview me," Kate said. "Right now?"

"I thought perhaps more privately," Judith said, reverting apparently to her nonreporter self.

"I'm at your service." Kate turned to Leighton. "And what are you doing in Greek these days?" she asked.

"Who does Greek before reading period?" Leighton reasonably inquired.

"Don't you go to class?"

"Of course. The professor drones on, and either I fantasize, or sleep, or write, depending on the conditions."

"But how do you pass the course?" Kate asked. "I have a feeling you've told me, but I suppressed it."

"Easy," Leighton said. "The exam covers one play."

"Yes."

"Well, I memorize it in reading period. Then I translate lavishly. I always get an *A*. And then I forget it."

"It sounds vaguely like a cobra digesting a pig," Kate said.

"That's Harvard," Leighton said. The dinner was over.

Two days later, while Kate was still at Dunster, the police reports, or a digest of them, were handed to Kate by a special messenger from Sylvia. Kate settled down to read them, ignoring as far as possible the banging on the stairs, the shouting, the music played at a decibel rate dangerous to human hearing. She had equipped herself with a small radio over which she heard the outpourings of the Harvard radio station, a treat. They played music upon music, some rock, most classical. In exam time, Leighton had told her, and in reading period, they had orgies. "Orgies?" Kate had naturally asked. "Yes," Leighton had said, flinging her cape around her—they were walking—"orgies: Bach orgies; Mozart orgies; Dylan orgies. Forty hours at a time. Mostly your sort of stuff; it's considered easier to study to." So, though it was not yet orgy time, Kate had Beethoven as a background to the account of murder.

Emerging from the perusal of this strange document some time later, Kate decided that the police, for all their efforts, which were many, knew little more than she did. They had not traced the source of the poison, but considered the fact significant: someone had had it for a long time, or acquired it very much elsewhere.

The victim had resided (no one in police reports ever lives, Kate thought) in an apartment on the top floor of a large private Cambridge house, owned by Harvard; a dean of Harvard and his family occupied the rest of the house. The apartment was wholly separate, with its own entrance, but it had not been lost on the police that the family of the dean included a daughter devoted to photography complete with darkroom. Also, the house had a large garden which, being searched, revealed ancient cans of pesticide containing cyanide. The police did not think the poison had been acquired from either of these sources, but the photographic stuff was still a possibility, if a distant one. What the police suggested was the cyanide had been readily available in World War II and after to those in various secret forces, on special missions, those likely to be captured by the enemy. Example: if a man was flying over territory he should not be flying over, and his plane developed trouble forcing him to land, he was supposed to take the poison, allowing the plane then to crash and burn, leaving the enemy with nothing. The cyanide was carried in capsule form, and had been widely issued at various times. Hermann Goering had managed to have the poison smuggled to him in prison despite having been searched, and committed suicide at Nuremberg just before he was to be

hanged. Many members of the armed forces were given
it unofficially, or at any rate had access to the capsules.
The upshot of all this was that there was a good bit of
the stuff lying around. "How wonderfully helpful,"
Kate said to herself.

There was no question that it was cyanide: the postmortem had established that. Even when Kate had arrived, the characteristic smell of burnt almonds still
hung around the body. The postmortem had established
as well the fact that the body had been moved after
death; soon after death. Rigor had not been interfered
with, had indeed begun before she was placed in the
men's room, they had concluded. As to where she had
taken the stuff, there was no clue. Anyone could have
handed it to her in a glass of strong-tasting drink, and
then washed and wiped the glass. Someone might, it
was surmised, have held her and forced the poison
down her throat, but she would have struggled, and
there were no signs of struggle.

The question of how a body had been moved without
anyone's noticing had been gone into by the police with
a thoroughness equaled only by the futility of the results. Since the body had been found in the morning,
the assumption was that it had been moved in the dark
of night, probably between three and six in the morning, apparently the only time when Harvard came anything like close to being deserted. Kate had once returned to the Faculty Club, in her early days in the attic
room, very late and it had been one of the eerier expe-
riences in a not-uneventful life. One let oneself in with
a key. No one was about. The large ancient building
creaked and groaned. Sounds echoed. Clearly, one
could have carried anything anywhere unnoticed.

Keys to Warren House had been no use as evidence:
too many were about, could have been reproduced at
any time. Still, the possession of such a key was certainly suggestive, pointing to a member of the English
Department, a restricted group, which must have been
an uncomfortable thought. The secretaries had been

closely questioned (I bet they were, Kate said to herself nastily).

Death from cyanide is painful, and very, very fast. There is no turning back. That, of course, was why men in services which might require a fast death, carried it. There was a description of cyanide attached to the report which Kate scanned: the special odor of cyanide, also known as hydrocyanic acid or prussic acid, remains detectable around the body for some time. The action is extremely swift, agonizing but swift. (So, Kate muttered to herself, I have gathered.) Breathing becomes difficult, followed by convulsions, muscular paralysis and death. All this happens within seconds. A cruel death, but the murderer could know that no help could come in time. The poison had been given in an alcoholic drink. But had the victim quaffed the drink? The mixture may simply have been strong enough to guarantee that one mouthful was sufficient. But that suggested a dose larger than one capsule.

Why the men's room? When all suggestions of imputation to the woman professor as unwelcome to a hitherto all-male department had been considered, and the police thought these fanciful (Kate snorted), the main fact was that the men's room had two obvious advantages. It was accessible to many people; it was on the first floor, while the ladies' room was on the second floor—the police understood that the victim had been assaulted in that room on a previous occasion, but had not met with bodily harm. (Kate offered a comment on what the police understood that was neither complimentary nor ladylike.) Finally, the men's room was less likely to be used as early as the ladies' room, the earliest in the office being the secretaries; the chairman, placement officer and others arrived later, some days not at all.

The police had interviewed those in any way connected with Professor Mandelbaum, including those who had attended the first party which had resulted in the bathtub incident, and all those who had had any connection with the victim before she came to Harvard

and were at Harvard at the time of the murder. These
included her former husband, "Moon" Mandelbaum,
from whom she had been divorced for over twenty
years: their simultaneous arrival at Harvard was declared to be a genuine coincidence; and Kate Fansler,
who had known the victim when they were graduate
students. Also interviewed were: the family in whose
house the victim lived in a rented flat on the top floor,
they knew little of their tenant, who had a separate entrance; all the members of the Harvard English Department who, to a man, expressed nothing but admiration
for the victim and profound regret at her death (Kate
made a rude noise). They said that she had been doing
a fine job. The secretaries at Warren House said the
same, more or less. Also interviewed were professors in
other departments who had met the victim in one ca-
pacity or another. Apart from certain students, social
connections, also interviewed were Luellen May, an occupant of an all-woman commune in Cambridge; Howard Falkland, who had been present at the party at
Warren House aforementioned; John Lightfoot, who
had known Luellen May years ago in Harvard College;
the woman who cleaned the victim's apartment. Not exactly a full roster of suspects, Kate sadly thought, particularly since the likeliest, some member of the English
Department in the higher ranks, was not, Kate guessed,
being seriously considered.

And it was, Kate realized that she had to admit, reluctant as she was to do so, mildly unlikely that any
member of the English professional staff, of whom Kate
had met only Clarkville, had really done it. They would
have settled for a slower death, and not so physical a
one. They had only to treat Janet with disdain and distance, to undercut her by indicating to students that
support for her was not the fastest way to appreciation
in the right quarters, and slowly Janet would have retired from the scene. Why bring about all this publicity?

Suppose, however, Kate mused, that some department at Harvard, fearing it would be the next to get a

woman professor through an endowed chair, decided to murder this one and scotch the whole scheme. Might they have dumped the body on Warren House and hoped for the best? But which department would it be? So many departments had never had a tenured woman that really, one would have to suspect the whole Harvard faculty. And I do, Kate thought, I do.

A note at the end of the police report said that transcripts of interviews were available to properly authorized . . . etcetera. In short, Kate said to herself, we are nowhere. Harvard is going to get away with it again. You, Kate said to herself, are getting downright silly about this place. What has Harvard ever done to you, except to let you into its Institute at Radcliffe, a damn fine place?

And, indeed, Kate thought the next morning in her study, it *was* a damn fine place. If women felt unwelcome elsewhere, they did not feel unwelcome here. And furthermore, Kate admonished herself, looking out of her window, Harvard knew how to do things. A crew of men was getting rid of snow. The grounds were beautifully kept. For graduation, Leighton had told Kate, they blow grass all over the Yard, yes, *blow* it, it gets all over everything but it works, there are lovely lawns soon after. Kate could hardly wait to see. If Leighton graduated, if Kate stayed that long, if life went on.

A knock on the door revealed an again disgruntled receptionist; this time, however, her irritation and bad manners were diluted ever so slightly by awe.

"Another call?" Kate timidly asked.

"You guessed it," the receptionist said, turning on her heel.

"Male, of course," Kate said, but softly. If Clarkville has found another body, Kate thought grimly, he can jolly well find someone else to talk to about it.

But it was Moon. He had been arrested for the murder of Janet, he had one call, did Kate think she could find bail and a lawyer before too long? If not, of course he would understand, he had been in jail before in the South and on peace marches, but he just thought he would let her know.

"In case you wondered," Moon said, "I didn't do it."

Chapter 8

In fact, I sometimes think only autobiography is literature.
VIRGINIA WOOLF

KATE HAD ONCE, while living in the Berkshires during a long-ago summer, had reason to call upon a Boston lawyer. He had been at Harvard Law School with Reed, he was a criminal lawyer, and Kate decided to call on him again for assistance. It was, of course, hard to make sudden inroads into the life of a busy man, a busy lawyer, but they had remained friends since that time, she and Reed had married, and he might now rally round even if Reed were in Lhambamamba.

"I might have known it," John Cunningham said when Kate got him on the phone. "That brouhaha at Harvard, that imbroglio with the first woman professor. Why didn't I know at once you were involved? After all, I knew you were in the area, but I should have been suspicious even if you weren't. Who's in jail now? Not Reed, I hope."

"No," Kate said, "Reed is on an advisory police tour. I'm alone in this, but a friend has been arrested for the murder."

"Any connection with the victim?" Cunningham asked.

"No," Kate said. "Except that he used to be married to her ages ago."

"EXCEPT!" Cunningham nearly shattered Kate's eardrum. There was a pause while Cunningham consulted his calendar and his secretary. "Can you come to my office?" he asked. "We'll see what we can do about getting bail set. They shouldn't have arrested him, I'm fairly sure of that, they wanted to take the heat off. I trust he hasn't been in jail before. No record?"

"Well," Kate reluctantly said, "he marched in the South with Martin Luther King, and later in peace marches. I rather think he has been in jail." Kate was annoyed at herself for sounding apologetic.

"Excellent," Cunningham surprisingly said. "Excellent. We'll establish prejudice, misuse of records, something. Not to worry. Come ahead, my good woman, come ahead. You know where I am."

When, in the fullness of time and legalities, Moon had been released on bail and was sitting, with Kate, in Cunningham's office, Cunningham, who had been alternately businesslike and reassuring with Kate, was decidedly astringent with Moon. Kate, eying Moon across the room, and realizing that he was unlikely, as a type, to appeal to Cunningham, tried to face the fact that it was within the realm of possibility that he was a murderer, or at any rate, that he had killed Janet. Kate's dismissal of this fact was, she knew, wholly personal: she could not, so many years ago, have felt a deep attraction to a murderer, let alone (Kate groaned to herself) have made love to him in the intervening years. Could Moon, Kate wondered, eschewing her own personal problems, have got embroiled in a hideous marital, or postmarital brawl with Janet and lost his inevitable cool?

Cunningham's mind was clearly working along the same lines, but without any personal need to find the man innocent.

"But what motive am I supposed to have had?" Moon asked.

"Who cares about motive," Cunningham shouted. "I don't; the police don't. The police care about opportunity and means. And even if they cared about motive, once you've been married to a woman you're considered to have a motive."

"If marriage is a sufficient motive for murder . . ." Kate began.

"Oh, Kate, do keep quiet. You know perfectly well what I mean. Most people are murdered by their relatives anyway, with husbands and wives, past or present, having the edge. My point is, you don't need a long-thought-out motive, all you need is a hot fight and a lot of bitter memories and recriminations."

"Well, we didn't have a fight," Moon said, "hot or cool, and there were no recriminations. I barely spoke to her, the one time we met. There wasn't anything to talk about."

"You seem to have found plenty to talk about with Kate."

"That's different," Moon said. "I've always loved Kate. I think I loved Kate when I married Janet."

"We all love Kate," Cunningham answered. "I'm sure it's because Kate is so lovable that I spend the greater part of my professional life bailing her academic friends out on charges of murder. I take it, however, that Kate was not the reason you came to Harvard, whereas Janet may well have been—don't interrupt me, we've got to see this as the police see it—and you were probably as surprised as I was to discover that Kate was at Harvard."

"Well," Moon said, "not exactly."

"What in God's name does that mean, 'not exactly'? I want the whole story, Mr. Mandelbaum, I want it in order, and I want it now. NOW!"

"Me too," Kate said.

"You keep quiet," Cunningham said. "Kate, you must see that the D.A.'s office is going to want a conviction on this one, if it comes to trial. We've got to make sure the police haven't got a good case. Right at the moment they've got a damn good case, and lots of money, your money. So please, shut up."

"I'll try. But if I think of a really intelligent question, I can ask it, can't I?"

"Damn it, yes. But let's get on with this. Now, Mr. Mandelbaum."

"I wish you'd call me Moon. Everybody does."

"I am not everybody. I am an exceedingly expensive criminal lawyer. Are you a Ph.D.? I'll call you Dr. Mandelbaum."

"Mr. will do," Moon said.

"But you do have a Ph.D.?"

"I do."

"You are, in fact, a professor? Not impersonating one? No fantasy life we ought to be dealing with here?"

"Plenty of fantasy life, but not about being a Ph.D. I am one, Kate can testify to that. I am a professor. I run a writing program in Minneapolis."

"I wish to God you had stayed there running it," Cunningham said.

"I don't," Moon said. "In spite of all this, I don't."

"Shall we," Cunningham said, "get back to opportunity and means? That is, unless you want to talk about the beauties of Harvard."

"I did have the means," Moon said. "At least, I might have had."

"What do you mean you had the means?" Kate said.

"Shut up, Kate."

"Yes, sir."

"What I mean," Moon said, "is that I had access—I believe that's the word—to cyanide in the army. In World War II. The Philippines. I had more than access, if you want the whole truth, and I know, I know, you do. You know, you should relax more. Try to be a bit more mellow."

"I AM NOT MELLOW!" Cunningham shouted, unnecessarily, Kate could not help reflecting. "I didn't know they were all that mellow in Minneapolis."

"Sorry," Moon said. "It wasn't hard to keep anything after that war. Probably after any war. Soldiers are always ripping things off, from their own outfit, from the enemy, everything. Anyway, I saw a bit too much and frankly I wanted the means of surcease, in case the memories got too bad."

"Had you been allotted the stuff?"

"Oh, yes. We were in the spearhead of the attack.

We knew what happened if we were caught, or lost. There was plenty of stuff around anyhow. I had it, I can't deny I had it."

"Who knew you had it?"

"That's the question, I realize. When I first got out, first got back home, perhaps some people knew. I don't think anyone's known for years. I don't think, to tell you the truth, that anyone ever knew. But I couldn't swear to what I may have said in those early days, right after I got back."

"You went to graduate school."

"Yes. That was quite a bit later. After I recovered. I wanted to study drama; tragedy. It seemed worthwhile. I met Kate there."

"I have gathered that. Kate, did you know he had cyanide?"

"No. I didn't know, not till this minute."

"Did you bring cyanide with you to Harvard?" Cunningham asked.

"Of course not," Moon said. "Why on earth would I? Well, I can see that's a silly question in view of the police case."

"And you had no idea your ex-wife, Janet, would be here when you came?"

"None. I know that's a sticky point, but it's true. Janet had no trouble believing it. As I said to Kate, even if someone noticed that two professors new to Harvard had the same last name, when it's Mandelbaum, well, they think, what's so surprising about two Mandelbaums in the Boston area?"

"In fact," Cunningham said, "there are only about half a dozen Mandelbaums in the Boston phone book. Look for yourself. What there are pages of are Connollys and Kellys. You've got your ethnics mixed."

"Janet didn't know I was coming; I didn't know she was here. We met only once at Harvard."

"Did you have a conversation?"

"Short and formal."

"Can you remember anything she said?" Cunningham asked.

"Yes. She said, apart from the usual amenities and insincerities, 'It's funny, Moon. I was the golden girl in graduate school, and you were a truculent arguer. I wrote an important book, and you played the guitar. But all the same, you fit in here better than I do. Isn't that funny?' "

"And what did you say?" Cunningham asked.

"I said that maybe they found it easier to relate to me, as a male and so on, but I sure didn't feel that I fitted in, whereas she seemed to me always to have held the same ideals as Harvard. I tried to say it kindly."

"And what did she say?" Cunningham's rapid questions reminded Kate, not unnaturally, of a cross-examination.

"She said she thought she had held the same ideals too. She said that bitterly. Then we separated. It was at a dinner honoring Eudora Welty, who had given a reading. I wouldn't have gone otherwise, hating these things, but I greatly admire Eudora Welty's work."

"Mr. Mandelbaum. If we could, for just one moment, abandon the delights of literature, drama, and Eudora Welty, will you tell me why you weren't exactly surprised to see Kate at Harvard? Had she told you she was coming?"

"No. She didn't know I was here."

"No, I certainly didn't," Kate said as Cunningham looked toward her. "He turned up at my study in the Institute one day, just after Janet had come apart in my hands. And a sight for sore eyes he was too."

"How did you know she was there?" Cunningham asked Moon.

"I had seen it in the *Gazette*, as I told her. But I knew before. The truth is, in a way, I sort of arranged it."

"Arranged it!" Kate exclaimed.

"Kate, my dear," Cunningham acerbically said, "if you would not keep exclaiming in that charming girlish manner, and repeating every syllable Mr. Mandelbaum utters, we *may* manage to get some facts into order before darkness is upon us. What did you arrange, Mr. Mandelbaum?"

Moon heaved a sigh. "You'll never forgive me," he said to Kate, "and it was all really accidental at first. Completely. You see, I had a friend from the peace march days who wanted to go to New York to see her brother. Well, she and I met one day in Central Square and we chatted a bit, she was living in a commune which I'd heard about, and she told me about this odd incident at Harvard and how one of her friends, whom I'd also known, was in this custody case and had met Janet in a bathtub—well, eventually it turned out that Janet had mentioned Kate to this woman who had mentioned it to the woman I met who wanted to go to New York to see her brother, so—well, I rather persuaded her to persuade Kate to come up and help them out, about Janet and all."

"Moon!" Kate said. "You know Jocasta!"

"Not well," Moon said. "But I admire her."

"John," Kate quickly said, "don't ask who Jocasta is. Please don't. All Moon is saying, really, is that he helped the wheels to turn."

"I thought," Moon said, "if it worked out that way, I'd like to see you again. I don't think I'm the sort who makes wheels turn."

"For someone all that mellow, you seem to have made plenty of wheels turn," Cunningham said. "You seem to have done just fine. What else have you got to confess, before I throw both of you out of here?"

"That's about it, really," Moon said. "But the police found out about the cyanide, and that Janet and I had once been married, and that I didn't have an alibi for any part of the time, so they arrested me. I suppose my having been a 'troublemaker' in the past helped their case, as they saw it."

"You sum up very well, Mr. Mandelbaum. Just one more question. Where, as far as you know, is that cyanide now?"

"I suppose it's back in Minneapolis in a locked metal

box I keep it in, together with a few other things. It's been there for over thirty years."

"You haven't ever removed it, and as far as you know, no one else has?"

"That's right."

"You would be willing, not that you have much choice, to have the cyanide checked on?"

"I'd be willing, but I'd rather it wasn't the police. I'm not mightily trusting of the police. They're as likely to plant evidence as to find it. But if you know someone you can trust . . ."

"I hope you don't go around, Mr. Mandelbaum, expressing such opinions of the police. It won't help your case."

"I won't. But I can tell you what I think, can't I?"

"Alas, yes. Would you mind waiting outside a minute while I have a word with Kate?"

"Not a bit. And thank you, Mr. Cunningham."

"It's Kate you've got to thank. I only hope that thanks will be the response in order when we're done."

When Moon had gone, Cunningham came around to the front of his desk and leaned against it, looking at Kate.

"I'm about to be warned," Kate said, taking out a cigarette.

"You are," John said, lighting it for her. "How well do you know Moon?"

"Very well in some ways, not at all well in others. What do I mean by that? I know the sort of person he is—all right, look dubious, I think I know the sort of person he is; obviously, when we think that, we are sometimes wrong. But I don't know how his life works on a day-to-day basis. When we were in graduate school I saw him almost every day, we studied for our exams together, we argued about Henry James, I liked him and Moon didn't. I had a sense of how his life went as far as work was concerned. I don't have that sense anymore. But if you told me that Moon had leaped on a motorcycle and run over a child, or gone hunting for deer, or assaulted a woman, I wouldn't believe you, I wouldn't, if you prefer, think it likely."

"How about growing enraged at a former wife and killing her?"

"For a smart lawyer," Kate said, "you sometimes ask very obvious questions."

"For a smart professor of literature, you sometimes fail to ask them. You've only his word for it at the moment that he and Janet did not meet, did not argue, did not have any problems between them. He had it all, means, opportunity, and if we can find it, probably motive. I just ask that as you go off like a friendly bloodhound on the scent, you bear all that in mind."

"Would you like to take a guess at what the motive might have been?"

"I never guess. It's a waste of time. I'm already checking to see that the divorce actually was a divorce, and not a friendly separation that has come apart. I'm also checking to see what the divorce settlement was: maybe someone agreed to something and has reneged. But even if all that checks out, and I'm fairly sure it will because whatever Mr. Mandelbaum is he isn't dumb, that doesn't mean he didn't have a motive we don't know about. Maybe she was about to tell you that when they were married he would only have sex dressed as a female Apache waving a tomahawk and hanging from the chandelier. Maybe he didn't want you to know that."

"John, you continue to amaze me. What a mind you have!"

"You just keep yours open, my dear. Don't stare so hard in another direction that you let someone creep up behind you. You're not in love with him, are you? All right, I see you're not, but do at least be sensible, which I'm convinced, underneath your dotty exterior, you are."

"I am usually called soignée," Kate said, rising with dignity to her feet. "Not dotty. What a word."

"Kate, my good woman, watch yourself. And keep in

touch. I'll let you know what we find about the divorce, and so forth. You tell me, I'll tell you."

"Thanks, John. Without you, of course, we'd all be helpless."

"I'll say this for you, Kate. You manage to hear what a man means and not only what he says. I admire that."

Kate, confused as always at a compliment, took a silent exit. From a phone booth downstairs, she called Leighton and asked her to send Judith around for that interview the next morning, if possible. Leighton asked if she could come too, and was firmly told that if she wanted to be a reporter she should join a newspaper. "I have reverted to being a difficult aunt," Kate said, and hung up. Dotty, indeed.

Judith duly presented herself at Kate's study at the Institute the next morning. "This is really great of you," she announced. "The paper said they'd be glad to print the interview, your views of women at Harvard, everything. They were very impressed that you sent for me."

"I sent for you," Kate said, "from ulterior motives. I'll be fair; you shall have your interview. But first, I'd like to interview you—about your interview with Janet Mandelbaum. Is that agreeable?"

"Oh, wow," Judith said, "I hope I can remember. I never even got to write it up before she was dead, what with one thing and another, and they couldn't have used it anyway."

"Well, that's good luck for me, because I'd rather just hear you tell me what she said, and you said, as you remember it. Don't try to put it in sensible order. I know how, when one remembers something that happened a while ago, one remembers it in bits and pieces, and something reminds you of something else you left out. Just ramble."

"Can I use a tape recorder with you so that I can really remember?"

"All right, though I hate the beastly things. So, I gather, did Janet."

"She wouldn't let me use one. I did ask. She seemed

afraid it would be used against her in some way. She didn't trust me."

"It's not so much a matter of trust as a question of judgment. But if you agree to let the person see the transcript and correct it, and have the tape back, I don't see why there should be a problem."

"She just seemed afraid," Judith said. "Not afraid, exactly. Anxious. Not giving anyone a chance to take advantage of her. Suspicious. I don't know what the right word is. Anyway, I was only allowed to take notes. I'd have brought them if you had told me."

"Just try to remember. You see, what may matter to me may not have seemed important for an interview in the paper. Not that I know what that might be."

"Oh, wow," Judith said. "I've got a class at eleven."

"If we don't get to me today, we will as soon as you can come back. I promise. How did the interview come about? Start at the beginning, get in all the details, even silly ones, and don't worry about boring me. Take full advantage: you may never get such a chance again."

"Gosh. Well, I called her in her office and told her my name and that I was on the *Independent*, and could we do an interview, and she said, like I told you at dinner that night, why?, and I said, because she was a new professor and a woman, and she said what did her being a woman have to do with it? and I said, well the new chair, and she said, well, I could come after her office hours if I wanted so I went. She had an office in Widener. We had that bit about the tape; I've just told you. She asked me my major, and I said bio anthro and she asked me about sociobiology which everyone does because Harvard is so split on that, and she asked which side I was on, and I said I wasn't with the socio-biologists, and she said she was, at least having read that altruism was in the genes to preserve the species, and I knew what that meant, because you can pretty well tell how people think by how they respond to sociobiology. Are you following this?"

"Closely," Kate said. "I think I understand. Put it this way: the sociobiologists believe it's all in the genes, determined before birth, programmed. Obviously this means, among other things, that it's no good thinking you can make people smarter than they are born to be. On the other side are those who believe also in the importance of social and cultural factors, and the possibility of change. Professor Mandelbaum was with those who think it's all in the genes, predetermined."

"Right, more or less. Anyway, I didn't argue much, since I wanted to encourage her to talk to me, so I brought up how great it seemed to us to have an English woman professor, since we'd never had one before, and of course half the Ph.D.'s go to women. She looked annoyed."

"Annoyed?"

"Well, sort of irritated. She said sure they wanted a woman, but she had been picked for her scholarly achievements, and that's what anyone should be interested in. So I asked her about them because she wanted me to. It was all the same stuff given out by Harvard when she was appointed, so I asked how Harvard compared with where she'd been before, trying to get her off her scholarly achievements. She said she didn't know yet. But, yes, she did say that people where she'd been didn't keep harping on her being a woman the way they did at Harvard. She said there have always been great seventeenth-century women scholars. Rosamund somebody, and Helen somebody, I think, and . . ."

"Rosamund Tuve, Helen White, Marjorie Hope Nicolson."

"Oh, wow," Judith said. "So then I asked about women's studies, and she said they were nonsense, absolute nonsense, a fad, there was no such thing, one was only interested in good poetry. As you can see, I guess, the interview wasn't exactly going great. So then I asked her about Cambridge, how she liked living in Cambridge. Leighton always says Cambridge is so great and leafy, so I asked her if she liked it because it was leafy. She saw what I meant by leafy, I guess, but she hated Harvard Square, the traffic, and the mess from doing over the subway, and all the kids, and the noise,

and the groups and couples—she said everyone was in
groups or couples—and nobody was serious. She had
thought students at Harvard would be serious. Are you
sure you're interested in all this?"

"Go on."

"Then she said I shouldn't write that down, and I
said I hadn't, and that what we'd been hoping for was
something about how she felt about the chair, and—
well, we just started going around again. She mentioned
the Zemurray-Stone chair, and said why didn't I go interview the present holder of that, who was a great
scholar too, and not keep harping on her. And then I
said, but Professor Mandelbaum, it matters a lot to us
serious women students to have a new role model like
you. We study here, we pay the same as the men, we
work as hard, we get better grades, but when we look
up at the faculty, there are hardly any women."

"And she said," Kate added, as Judith paused for
breath, "that there would be if any women were good
enough."

"Right. And she also said that we could go to wom-
en's colleges if that was what we wanted, and that she
never wanted to hear the phrase 'role model' again.
You know though," Judith added after a moment, "I've
heard this sort of thing before; I mean, plenty of
women talk that way, like when I was a kid there were
people who were glad their kids could play in the Little
League and all where before only boys could, but all
the same they'd tell you they weren't 'libbers.' I mean,
nothing she said was new, though it was kind of depressing to hear it all over again from someone who'd
made it that way, but underneath it was different with
her."

"Different? How?"

"I don't know. Except that she could have turned the
whole discussion off. Other women do. I got the feeling,
well, not exactly that she *wanted* to argue with me,
but . . ."

"As though it were a sore tooth she kept poking with
her tongue, that sort of thing?"

"Well, it was, really, when you come right down to it, well, you know, I had the feeling she was lonely."

"Anything else said?"

"Not much. Oh, I could have worked something up for the paper, but the main news was going to be negative: 'new woman professor not a sister,' that sort of thing."

"Sounds like Margaret Thatcher."

"Exactly what the editor said."

"What still remains so mysterious to me," Kate said, "is what did she really want? From Harvard, and from her life here?"

"I think I know that," Judith said. "She talked of visiting here, before she really came, and of attending Clarkville's lectures on the Victorians. He gives them in Sanders Theater, you know, five hundred people, he's just a marvelous lecturer."

Kate pondered, not for the first time, on the mysteries of the human personality. Meeting Clarkville in the SCR of Adams House, not to mention at Warren House, who would have guessed he was a marvelous lecturer?

"I think she hoped to be like that," Judith continued. "But of course she never could, not at Harvard. The students all shop around the first week of classes, lots of them dropped into her class out of curiosity, but very few took it. She didn't seem that interesting, and she wanted papers."

"The students here are a snotty lot," Kate said. "Did she mention all this?"

"No; I heard it from students. Leighton even dropped in. Dullsville, she said."

"Not Clarkville," Kate sadly noted.

Chapter 9

Miss ———, in this undertaking, appeared to shrink from no effort; resorting largely, whenever the opportunity offered, to the natural expedient of interrogation.
HENRY JAMES
The Portrait of a Lady

KATE AND SYLVIA had lunch in Sylvia's apartment, George having awoken to another dawn of departure. Kate, as she told Sylvia with a sigh, was back with silence, away from the ambience of intense adolescence and its attendant noises. They sat in the living room gazing out at the river and eating yogurt out of containers.

"The horrible fact is," Sylvia said, having listened to Kate's account of her morning, "that Janet would probably have been happier in a harem, with only occasional visits from the sultan and all the hierarchies clearly marked. She's one of those women who like the world to rest steady beneath her glass, and the poor thing was destined to live and die in times when one couldn't even hold the glass, let alone focus it."

"And all that beauty," Kate said. "One of the lies I have always hated most about Charlotte Brontë was that she would have given all her talent to be beautiful. A man said that, of course, who knew nothing about it. I sometimes think homely women have a fine start in life: they know the rules, and how the game will be played. The early pain, the early lack of that marvelous ego satisfaction when all the men are gathered around like peacocks is well repaid later in life with accomplishment. But what young girl will believe that if you tell her? Why am I rambling on like this—I'm fading, Sylvia, Leighton says it's synapsis, and she's right. I guess I mean that Janet would have done better without brains or without beauty; with both she ended up not only lonely, but dead."

"Her brother is coming," Sylvia said, "to ship her things back home. She left a will with a lawyer back there, asking to be buried in the graveyard where her parents are, where she grew up. She has two brothers. Janet left all her money to their children, by the way. Would you like to meet the brother when he comes?"

"What I'd like," Kate said, "would be to look through Janet's rooms *before* the brother begins on them."

"That's probably not to be hoped for. The police have locked it up, so that the family in the house can't get to it, much to their annoyance. I think we had better try for simultaneity."

"I suppose the police have determined that she wasn't entertaining anyone before she died? That isn't where the poison was administered?"

"No evidence of that at all, I gather. Have you any other ideas? Because if not, I think we've got to face the fact that either Moon did it, which you deny, or someone from wholly impersonal motives did it, either to attack professional women or to save Harvard from professional women, which comes to exactly the same thing and is just a teeny bit unlikely, or—Kate, you've got to face this—that Luellen did it."

"Sylvia, Luellen had everything to lose from any more contact with Harvard. She'd got off by not telling the police she'd been called to the bathtub scene. The last thing she would want would be to get further involved."

"As far as you know, my dear. But from what you tell me of your conversation with her, she sounds pretty angry. Try to remember there's no one here at the moment but you and me. I can remember some radical feminists who came close to murder at public meetings when all they did was offend everyone, even their friends."

"That's pure stereotype, Sylvia, and you know it. If I have to pick a murderous stereotype, I'd rather pick Howard Falkland. Men are always writing books about murdering women—it's one of their favorite fantasies: revenge for having their prerogatives usurped: sexual prerogatives, political prerogatives, social prerogatives. . . ."

"You aren't facing up to Luellen with your usual objectivity, Kate, if I might mention it. If I were Luellen, I think I'd have badly wanted revenge on someone like Janet Mandelbaum, who'd got it all with never a thought for another woman."

Kate was silent for a time. "All I can say is that I've met Luellen and you haven't and I don't think women like Luellen kill other women. But I realize that isn't much of an answer for the police. Will you agree, anyway, to letting me play out the Howard Falkland end, at least for now?"

"Kate, love, it's not a matter of my being willing, just of you keeping an open mind. What 'play' did you have in mind?"

"I thought," Kate said, glad to return to a lighter tone, "that we might give a little dinner party here. Andy Sladovski and Lizzy, his wife, Penny Artwright and Howard Falkland. I thought we could just sit around and keep them talking."

"Maybe they won't come?"

"I'll put it to Andy that I madly want them to come. Falkland's the only one who won't come out of kindness, and he'll probably come because one doesn't refuse invitations from full professors, even women, even not from Harvard."

"You do it without me. What I keep wondering is, didn't Janet have any friends? She must have, mustn't she? Everyone does, don't they?"

"She had her male colleagues at the old university, and young male friends, ex-graduate students who courted and attended her. The truth is, Sylvia, it struck everyone as a bit odd that she should have asked for me out of the blue like that, but I think the fact is there wasn't anyone else. There may have been women friends back home, but not ones who would understand this problem."

"Kate, my dear," Sylvia said, with less than her usual flippancy, "if you want to know, friendship or the lack of it is going to be what it will all turn on in the end. Whether or not women change their lot will depend on their future friendships, what Virginia Woolf called something more varied and lasting because less personal."

"I like the way Louise Bogan put it too," Kate said, "if I know what you mean: something between love and friendship, expressed by a gesture that is not a caress."

Moon's arrest had made the newspapers, but this seemed, if anything, to have raised his stock with his writing class. At any rate, he had returned to it and suggested that, if anyone found the subject interesting, they write a story about it, first from the point of view of the student, and then from the point of view of the man arrested. A good writing exercise. He insisted to Kate, when they walked in the Mount Auburn cemetery in late February, that he hadn't killed Janet and that she, Kate, would have to find out who did. He doubted the police would get very far, but he admitted that he was not really open-minded on the subject of the police.

The police from Minneapolis had, on instructions from their Boston colleagues, gone to Moon's house, now sublet, and found the cyanide capsules where he had said they were. He said he had counted them when he moved there, and that number was still present. The police had confiscated the capsules, supposedly for the purpose of determining that the content was cyanide. Moon had said he wanted them back, they were his property. Cunningham guessed he was out of luck on that one.

Kate worried about the fact that she kept asking him

about Janet. The woman troubled and intrigued her and, somewhere, whatever Cunningham said, there had to be a motive for her murder. "What I want to understand is what went wrong with your marriage. The fact that you've had two wives since does rather suggest it wasn't altogether her fault."

"And the fact that you had, even as a callow youth, too much sense to marry me."

"I still don't see why you couldn't work it out. Didn't you want to try?"

"Not in the end, no. She kept wanting me to be something I wasn't: the sort of man her parents would have liked her to marry, I guess. Quietly dominating, successful, a good provider—you know the ideal better than I do, Kate."

"Then why did she marry you?"

"I've tried to say. In the beginning, I seemed able to master her. I only wanted her, I didn't want to run her life. You have to remember she was beautiful; men did want her."

"Why didn't anyone else try to master her for the same purpose?"

"I think she scared most men. She was too smart, and though she wanted to be ladylike, she couldn't help having very definite opinions about things. I rather liked that, of course, but then we both know how unusual I am." Moon grinned.

"Didn't she ever worry at all about your being here at Harvard? Sorry to keep going round and round; I don't know what I want to ask."

"She worried at first that I'd tell people about her; she always cared about what people thought. But I guess she realized I wouldn't. And then, the fact that other marriages of mine had failed rather took the blame off her. Kate, if I could tell you what you want to know, I would, you know; I would."

Kate had decided against a dinner party. It would have been a gracious return for her lovely dinner at the Sladovskis, but people, having eaten, tend to grow sleepy, their conversation diffuse and anecdotal. Whereas, if they arrive well after dinner, ready for the evening's second wind, so to speak, one could shape the conversation in some sort of intelligent way while plying Howard Falkland with liquor and provocation.

"Any instructions?" Andy had asked when they had discussed the evening.

"Since you so perspicaciously ask," Kate said, "yes. At some point, begin attacking Clarkville. Any aspect that occurs to you, but subtly. I'll join in somehow. Penny, I gather, hates him anyway."

"You realize you are endangering two promising careers at Harvard, if this gets back to the old boy."

"Oh, Andy, don't, then. We shan't even mention Clarkville."

"Kate, Kate, I'm joking. Howard will tell Clarkville what suits him, not what's said. I'm not staying at Harvard, Lizzy won't stand for it for one thing, and I can't stick the place, for another. As to Penny, Penny can watch out for herself, I'm pleased to say. You heard the story about the bridge game. Not to worry."

Sylvia's apartment, which one entered by walking up a short flight of stairs, made a dramatic impression. The large windows, with the river beyond, rescued the rather unimaginative modern design of the apartment and gave it style and drama. The furnishings were the best Danish modern, and Howard's defenses visibly relaxed once he saw he was in the presence of money. One would have had to dig very deep into Howard's psyche to get him to recognize any such thing, but it was evident to Kate, who had met the same response often before. Kate had found only one advantage to impressing people: it softened them up. Which was why her own surroundings were carefully not impressive. And not in Cambridge. For one moment, Kate thought longingly of her New York apartment, and Reed, and her abandoned office at the university. How did I get here? she thought. And then the evening began.

They had all arrived together, apparently at Howard's request. Kate wondered what his version of her was, part Clarkville, part Andy, with a bit of general gossip thrown in. Kate had taught long enough to know that one would find oneself unrecognizable in most students' descriptions and accounts of one's life and opinions. Fortunately, one seldom heard them. Kate decided she might as well begin with a discussion of student opinion of professors, how derived and how accurate.

"Which of us could bear to hear what is really thought of us?" Kate said, as she passed around drinks and what Sylvia called munchies. "For all our indifference, feigned or sincere, the initial shock would be overwhelming, wouldn't you think?"

"I was once in a ladies' room when some students came in and started to talk about me," Penny said. "It was a dreadful experience. I couldn't emerge, and they hung around for what seemed hours, combing their hair and talking in that idle way. It began to look as though I would have to emerge to universal embarrassment, when they finally bolted."

Kate was immediately aware of one thing: Howard was discomforted. Not only because Penny had mentioned the ladies' room, but because her glance at the other two women, that they might confirm her embarrassment, reminded Howard that he was in a room with three women and only two men, of whom he was one. The proportions were, for Howard, as unfortunate as they were unaccustomed. Everyone knew, or Howard thought everyone knew, that extra women were an embarrassment. Kate blessed Penny for a brilliant beginning.

"It just goes to show," Andy said, "how new you women are to the big time. Men have been checking out the stalls for years before taking a leak. The trouble with most women students is they don't really believe women professors actually exist, and they certainly don't believe they pee."

"Better than professors like Clarkville," Penny said, "who don't believe women professors think!"

"Penny," Kate said, "don't you think you're a little hard on Clarkville? I've just learned he gets five hundred students for his lectures on the Victorians. I call that impressive."

"Oh, he's impressive as a lecturer, all right," Penny said, "and even as a scholar. He reads all the languages George Eliot read, which is no mean accomplishment, and he's even followed her footsteps when she and Lewes were following Goethe's. Clarkville is great at dipping deeper and deeper into the same material. What he can't do is imagine it might be any different. He can't really imagine what it might have been like to be George Eliot."

"Could any man?" Lizzy asked.

"Oh, yes; some could. Look at Joseph Barry on George Sand. Clarkville doesn't want to. I think he deems it a great pity George Eliot was a woman at all. She had such a *masculine* mind."

"Say what you want," Howard rejoined, "I've been one of his section men long enough to know that those kinds of lectures are pure genius. If you think you could do better, you're welcome to try, either of you"—this was directed at Andy and Penny, but was intended, Kate felt, for herself also.

"I for one wouldn't want to," she said. She got up and poured more drinks for everyone. As she handed Howard his bourbon and water, she had the impression that he was coming to the boil. She rather guiltily hoped so.

"I'm not denigrating his talents," Andy said. "But let's face it. That course is a Harvard tradition. Everyone knows the kind of exam there'll be, and no papers, and if you butter up your section man, or woman, well, *they* correct the exams. I admit people keep coming to the lectures because they're entertaining as hell, even moving."

"Let us not forget," Penny said, "the day when Clarkville got detained somewhere, and told his only woman section man to take over the lecture, and when she got up on the podium and announced herself and her intention, most of the audience simply left."

"That wasn't Clarkville's fault," Howard said, down-ing his bourbon.

"Help yourself," Kate said, pointing to the table of drinks. Howard rose to do so.

"He certainly never said a word about it to the class later on," Andy said. "He could have bawled them out, or given a little lecture on courtesy and so forth, but he never did. Don't tell me he didn't know what had happened. And why pick the woman for the job anyway?"

"If he hadn't you'd have said he was discriminating against women," Howard said. "You can't ever win with people like you."

"You didn't think Clarkville should have said something later?" Andy asked.

"No, I don't. It was her chance and she muffed it."

"Do you think they would have stayed for you?" Lizzy asked. There was no hostility in the question; she was curious.

"I don't think quite as many people would have left," Howard said, "if you want the truth. Perhaps we'll find out sometime."

"I'm sure Clarkville will be glad to arrange it for you," Andy said. "You seem rather a favorite of his."

"Why the hell shouldn't I be?" Howard asked. "What's with you two, anyway. What have you got it in for me about?"

Since Kate thought it likely that either, or both, were about to tell him, she interceded. "I think," she said, "they wonder about your part in getting Janet Mandel-baum landed in the bathtub."

"Why should I have had anything to do with it?" he asked.

"Because," Lizzy said, "you were there."

"How do you know I was there?"

"Because I told her you were," Kate said. "Luellen May told me. She said John Lightfoot had introduced you earlier."

Howard groaned. "I've been trapped. You invited me here to trap me."

"That's only partly true," Kate said. "I invited you because I wanted to meet you. I heard your paper the other night, and I have a certain admittedly well-controlled interest in the Harvard English Department. After all, I'm in an English Department myself, and comparisons are always enlightening. But the fact that you were at that party, and that Janet is now dead, were also motives and I don't deny it."

"You seem fairly skillful, all of you together, in demonstrating that I disagree with the lot of you on most things." Howard poured himself another drink and was clearly, Kate saw, bent on demonstrating that he was one of those who become more self-revealing and truculent in their cups. "Well," he went on, "I do disagree, or assume I do. So you've got me trapped in a room of women's libbers. O.K., I'm still a male chauvinist pig. I think women are happier when they're looking up to some man, and having kids, which is what nature intended them for."

"But you don't mind them paying to be your students," Penny said.

"Of course they should be educated like men; they have to live with men, though some of them don't seem to think so these days."

Kate looked upset, as indeed she was, that he had been driven to such petulant arguments so early in the discussion. That he became so angry so easily was certainly interesting. Lizzy apparently agreed, and began to talk to Howard. It intrigued Kate to notice that Howard listened to Lizzy with a willingness he showed toward no other woman. It was her manner, unthreatening, her gentleness, the fact that she was a nurse and not an academic and was thus both, presumably, womanly and nonintellectual.

"These are hard times for academics, Howard," she said. "I don't blame you, the others don't either, for being angry at having to face the competition of women now as well as of other men. Plenty of colleges are trying to hire women now; I know that."

"Then you know more than I do," Penny said. "Harvard isn't trying all that hard, and plenty of other places will tell you that they've got their woman, or have filled their quota, or whatever it is. Chairmen just like to tell men they don't hire that they had to hire a woman instead."

"I know, Penny," Lizzy said. "All the same, even Andy, even I get angry sometimes that there is even more competition for scarce jobs than there used to be. That's why working-class men don't love Blacks in the face of affirmative action. Howard's just expressing what a lot of men feel."

"Of course they do," Kate said soothingly, or so she hoped. One was either soothing by nature, like Lizzy, or not; yet, Kate thought, nobody ever blamed Lizzy for not being acerbic, witty, stimulating. We all want women who will nurture us, she thought. "But surely," she said, "putting something in Janet's drink was going a little far in undermining the competition, however tough things are. Besides, Janet wasn't really competition for you; quite the contrary, I should have thought. If they'd got their 'woman' as a full professor, they wouldn't be that eager to hire younger women."

"Look," Howard said, "you're getting this all wrong. I admit the way I acted may not have been admirable, but I wasn't out to get Janet, though I admit I did take advantage of the situation, well, some advantage. All right, I certainly shouldn't have given her a stronger drink than she wanted, I shouldn't have said she was a sister of Luellen's, but you act as though I slipped her a Mickey Finn."

"That's rather what we thought," Andy said.

"What the hell do you mean you thought?" Howard yelled. "You thought! What the hell do you mean?" Howard was now standing over Andy looking for action. Could he stay angry long enough to administer cyanide? To plan murder? Kate rather thought so. But perhaps, she cautioned herself, I want to think so.

"Howard," Kate said, "please sit down and talk to me. That's right, sit. Don't get angry. Just answer this question: Did you or did you not put anything in Jan-

et's drink that night at Warren House? The night of
the bathtub incident?" (Or any other night, she wondered.)

"Yes, I did. I put vodka into it. All right. But it isn't
as though I were undermining someone in Alcoholics
Anonymous. I mean, she wasn't drinking ginger ale, or
soda water, she was drinking Campari. I just added a
little hundred-proof vodka. All right, I shouldn't have. I
know that. I just wanted to see what she would do. I
must say, she exceeded my wildest expectations. She
passed out, well, got woozy anyhow, and went to the
ladies' room. That's all I had to do with it."

"Then what happened?" Kate asked. "Please, Howard, just tell us how it went, step by step, and I promise
we'll do our best to see that it's forgotten if it can be.
But you must see, we've got to find out, now that she's
been murdered."

Howard had reached the maudlin stage. He was now
at the point of confession and regret. Kate wished she
did not have to hear it. She did have to hear it.

"I was there with a girl," Howard said. "A graduate
student. Not a libber type. Actually, it was her idea,
and the others', to ask Janet. I guess they thought it
would be funny. Well, actually, it was their idea to
make her drink stronger. Not that I excuse myself, I
wanted to do it too. I suppose I vaguely thought Clarkville would be amused if she made a fool of herself.
When she, Janet, went to the ladies' room and was
clearly passing out, the girls went in and, well, they
lowered her into the tub. I think they really were scared
she might be, well, having a fit or something. She went
limp, I guess—look, you aren't going to try to get them
into this, are you? because, really, they were scared,
and they told me what happened, and I promised more
or less—"

"We won't get them involved if we can get to know
the whole story, the *whole* story," Kate said sternly.
Stern aunt role, she told herself, keep it up.

"Well, once she was lying in that enormous tub, they
turned the shower on hoping to bring her around, I

guess. I'm not sure they really thought it would work—look, the whole thing was stupid, sophomoric from beginning to end, but we didn't put any poison or anything in her drink, you've got to believe that. We didn't put anything in her drink but drink."

"What happened after that?"

"We got scared. I suggested breaking up the party, and everyone sort of cleared out."

"All of them thinking," Kate said, "that Professor Mandelbaum had passed out from drinking too much and was lolling in the bathtub?"

"Well, more or less, yes, I guess so."

"Commendable indeed. And then you decided to cap your achievement by calling Luellen."

"I hate lesbians," Howard said. "She told me she was in a custody fight, and I don't think lesbians should bring up kids. I'd had a hell of a row with her, it was awful, and had, well, made me really mad."

"That must have been as unusual as it was elevating," Andy said. Kate glared at him.

"So you thought, what fun, to get Luellen involved with this. She might get into trouble, Janet might get called a lesbian, and there would be fun and games all around. Is that about it?" Kate asked.

"You certainly have a clear-headed way of putting things," Penny said. "I admire it."

"When did you have this row with Luellen?" Kate asked.

"Oh, a while ago. We have a mutual friend. I dropped in once, when she was visiting him—they were catching up with old times. I don't know how it got started but it did. She blamed men for everything that was lousy in the world, and I lit into her. These women horrify me."

"Frighten you might describe it better," Penny said.

"O.K., they frighten me. What they need . . ."

"Don't say it," Kate interrupted, "I implore you. Let's try to end the evening on a fairly nonacrimonious note, if that is possible."

"What *you* need . . ." Penny said.

"PENNY!" Kate barked, very auntly.

"Well," Howard said, "that's all. I called Luellen from Warren House and said one of the sisters was in trouble."

"That she came to help a friend doesn't impress you?" Andy asked.

"Like those dumb broads in stories who are always getting trapped by the villain in deserted houses," Howard said.

"Is there anyone you'd go to the rescue of?" Andy asked. "Just asking for information."

"He'd go for Clarkville," Lizzy said. "Which everyone knows. So if someone wanted to trap Howard in a jam, they would say they were calling for Clarkville. One just has to know what to say, that's all."

"There is a difference," Penny pointed out.

"Which I suggest we do *not* explore," Kate said. "What chance do you think the Red Sox will have next season?"

"At Harvard," Andy said, "we discuss this year's game against Yale, or next year's. Who bothers with the Red Sox? Really, Kate!"

Chapter 10

THE DEAN in whose house Janet Mandelbaum had occupied the top floor was anxious to get her things
moved out so that he might find another tenant for the
apartment, but Janet's brother kept the dean waiting, as
Sylvia informed Kate, almost two weeks. Kate's feelings
about this delay were mixed. She was amused that Janet's brother should keep Harvard hanging upon his convenience, and that he refused to trust anyone in that
exalted institution to pack up Janet's things and ship
them home. He, her brother, represented the family
who were her heirs, and he intended to see that they got
what was coming to them. So, at least, Sylvia surmised,
since the police refused to open the apartment to anyone else.

The delay, which took them to the end of February,
was not unwelcome to John Cunningham. As he told
Kate, it gave them time to let the detectives he'd hired
dig up what evidence there was. Kate herself felt that
particular anxiety inherent in situations which ache for
a resolution and are prevented from achieving it. She
knew this anxiety to be dangerous in murder cases: it
led to precipitous conclusions and, all too often, to the
accusation of the wrong person. Thus Moon had been

arrested and, thanks to Cunningham, released. He was not, however, free from suspicion, though his rare mellowness of character prevented him, Kate was grateful to observe, from being gnawed at by anxieties.

With Luellen, it was not so easy. Having averted their eyes from Moon, the police had turned them hopefully upon her, and Kate, who dreaded Luellen's accusations and bitterness, forced herself nonetheless to spend time at the coffee house, offering Luellen, if not comfort, at least a safe object for her anger. Nor did Kate delude herself, even if her repeated assurances to the police had prevented them from taking any precipitous action with Luellen, that Luellen's anger was unjustified or undeserved by one like Kate who, it more and more seemed to her, had been blessed with a life outrageously felicitous.

All the same, Luellen's sarcastic attacks on Kate and Harvard were not easy to bear, nor was Luellen's constant tendency to consider Kate and Harvard as one guilty package. "Perhaps they've no respect for you because you're a woman," she would fling at Kate, "and a woman who may even now and then talk about feminism, but they find you a place at that Institute, you snap your fingers and there's a lovely apartment to live in, your relations have probably given Harvard millions, which certainly matters"—Kate uneasily wondered whether this was a guess or an ascertained fact— "how can you know what it's like to be questioned over and over and never believed, and made to feel like some sort of creep? What makes me so angry is that those policemen don't think of their families any more than they have to, maybe they talk to their children twenty-five minutes a day, I'm sure they screw around, but they have the right to preach about families as though they were all holy, and treat me as though I were scum."

"I wish you would let me find you a lawyer," Kate would repeat for the twentieth time, bracing herself for the inevitable refusal.

"Oh, great, Lady Bountiful does appeal to you as a

stance, doesn't it? The fact is, I'll probably never manage to pay the lawyer in the custody fight, let alone pay another one, and they all know how to hound you. And what good would it do anyway? I haven't killed that dreadful woman, I've never harmed anyone, and I don't need a lawyer to help me say so. If only the police would let me alone."

Through these discussions Joan Theresa, sitting uneasily by, would try to comfort Luellen with the fact that the police would probably do no more than harry her, that they had not arrested her as they had Moon; she did her awkward best to ease the atmosphere. The Maybe Next Time Coffee House seemed, in its air of tenuous hope, to have produced an ambience wholly suited to its wistful name. Only Jocasta, not by law allowed in a restaurant and therefore meeting Kate on the front stoop, remained comfortably herself.

Finally, Sylvia, whose deftness at pulling strings was becoming awesome, announced that the brother had arrived, was in Janet's apartment arranging for the move, and would be willing to greet Kate and let her look around under, it was clearly implied, his close supervision. Early in March, therefore, Janet's brother opened the door of Janet's apartment to Kate.

He was a hearty. That was evident from the first moment he reached a large hand out to Kate, and greeted her. It was the sort of hand that Kate secretly considered a paw, hairy, heavy, and barely prehensile. "Come in, Kate, come in. My name's Bill. I guess I can call you Kate, even if you are an important lady professor. After all, my sister was an important lady professor too, though I never could see what good it did for her. You're not bad looking either; why should either of you have wanted to mess around with all those professors, that's what I wonder."

"Yes, please call me Kate," Kate said. Getting used to this new rage for first names was something Kate was determined upon. But beyond that, she instantly recognized Bill as the sort of man who would have to be cajoled, played with in a manner Kate despised. She had already guessed that that large paw would soon be around her shoulder. It was. How the same womb could have produced this chap and Janet was certainly a wonder, but not one new to Kate's experience. Bill, in fact, went a certain way toward explaining Janet.

"I know you want to look over poor Janet's things before I pack them away," Bill said. "Some important Boston or maybe Harvard man called and told me that. It's a little difficult for me to see why a stranger should look through Janet's things before her family gets to them, but I guess we have to remember that poor Janet didn't die in the ordinary way. Where do you want to start, Kate?" Kate moved as gracefully as possible away from the encircling arm.

"I shan't be any more intrusive than necessary," she demurely said. "We can look together through her personal things if you would like." She hoped this didn't sound too inviting. "Frankly, I want first of all to get a sense of her from this place—a sense of the life she lived here," she added, in firmer tones. "It's been left as she left it that night, or morning, when she died, so I suppose the only change is dust and a stale atmosphere."

"Hell, yes," Bill said, throwing open a window. "I was about to do that even without you. Look at all those books," he said, turning in the room which was lined with bookcases. "They don't seem to have helped her much, do they?"

"Well," Kate said, "we can't know, can we?" She had often noticed that when people with large libraries fall into trouble, the fact that the books had not risen en masse to help them always seemed to give those without books comfort.

"The way it looks to me," Bill said, "is if she'd lived the life of a normal woman none of this would have happened. I'm all in favor of women working, of course, provided they put their homes and children first. And I do think that a woman who doesn't have children has missed the best part of life. Don't you?"

"Since, if I did, I should have to confess to having

missed the best part of life, you can hardly expect me to agree," Kate said, she hoped lightly.

"Well, some of you can't help it," Bill said. "Fellow I know, his daughter has had to have all her insides out, cancer, so of course she will have to adopt kids. It's the principle of the thing, isn't it? What is life without children, after all?"

Kate forbore telling him. Life with children had undoubtedly its great rewards, but Kate rather wished from time to time that parents would be silently appreciative of them: they had, rather, the air of trying to convince themselves of something. "I rather think," she said, "that Janet chose what she wanted. Perhaps it turned out to be more difficult than she thought it would be, but then sometimes raising children does too, doesn't it?"

"What I mean to say is, Janet was so intent on becoming an important professor, and then being invited to teach at Harvard—well, we were all impressed at home, I don't mind telling you. I said to my wife, 'Imagine old Janet at Harvard, all those boys, and she couldn't even put up with me and Nick when we were kids.' Nick's her other brother. When we were kids, Janet was always trying to run things and getting mad because she couldn't—she was the oldest, of course. 'Well,' my wife said to me, 'it certainly took a lot of determination to go as far as she did, and maybe it was because you made her so mad when she was a kid.' My wife says Janet made up her mind all men were thugs and goons, and I said well, she wasn't far wrong, was she?" Bill matched his speech with a small lunge which Kate neatly sidestepped.

"Janet wasn't made for marriage," Bill said, "and then when she got married she went and married a Jew. Not that we have anything against Jews, but after all, it does show something, doesn't it; like to like, I say; a girl shouldn't marry so far away from her family. I'd be darn mad if one of my daughters married a Jew and I don't mind saying so. To each his own, marriage is hard enough as it is."

"You may be right," Kate said. It was Mencken's answer to those who argued with him beyond the bounds of discourse. "Do you mind," Kate asked, with a deprecating smile, "if I just wander around and think?"

"Perhaps," Bill returned, "you won't have to think so much in the kitchen. We could start there. I don't want to take too long over this, I got plenty of important business waiting for me at home."

"Look," Kate said, "I'm sorry to be a nuisance. Let me just have a look in the kitchen, and then I'll leave it to you, if you want to pack up the pots and things. Is that all right?" Kate had little idea, certainly, what she might expect to find there, but nothing could be eliminated with so little to go on.

But the kitchen offered no clues. It had been designed as part of the living room, ideal for entertaining, but Kate, who was like that herself and able to recognize the symptoms, knew, when she saw it, the kitchen of someone with little interest in cooking. The over-equipped kitchen had not found an occupant who could properly appreciate it. The refrigerator contained almost nothing but a carton of, by now, stale milk, half a container of yogurt, other simplicities, all bought, Kate noticed, at Sage's, the elegant local store. There were no signs in the kitchen or living room of any visitor. True, any evidence might have been cleared away, but something about the echoing sounds, the extraordinary precautions that would have had to be taken to remove a body from this house—no, Kate felt it, Janet had not died here. More, one felt that she had not lived here.

"Sad kitchen, isn't it," Bill said, echoing these thoughts. "No sign of life. I like a kitchen with women in it cooking, and baking bread."

Kate dearly wanted to ask Bill to squat somewhere and let her, Kate, continue probing without this hulking male shadow, but the man had rights and probably half suspected Kate of trying to hide something or make off with it. The only thing Kate could find would be something no one else would think significant, but it hardly seemed worth the effort to explain all this to a man of Bill's sensibilities.

What interested Kate most in the living room was the books. The police had, Cunningham told her, been through the volumes to be certain nothing was hidden in or behind them—poison, for instance, or threatening letters—but they had returned them to their places, testifying to their innocence at least from these charges. Kate was, unlike Bill, surprised at how few books there were, few, that is, for a professor of English. Professors of literature collect books the way a ship collects barnacles, without seeming effort. A literary academic can no more pass a bookstore than an alcoholic can pass a bar. Yet there was no evidence of this here. Janet's books on the seventeenth century were many: she had clearly brought them all with her, and had received a few recent ones, perhaps for reviewing. Well, no doubt such signs of intellectual life, the sort of signs that survive death, would be in the study.

Yet this was not so. The apartment had two bedrooms, one of which Janet had made her study. Her typewriter, covered, stood on the large table which served her as a desk. There were two wire baskets holding papers and letters: papers to be read, letters to be answered. Kate knew the system. As an academic without a personal secretary, one was either a happily unorganized animal, making large piles all over one's desk and other spaces, piling up unanswered and frequently unopened mail, waiting for a brief respite to "clean off one's desk." Or, like Janet and Kate, one kept up with it, organizing the necessary work in a provocative way: one wanted to get it done. Yet even here, Kate wondered. Janet was behind on her letters, through which Kate flipped as Bill glared. Letters of recommendation, letters needed for tenure reviews—they were overdue at Janet's death. Kate guessed this was uncharacteristic. Perhaps it was the rush of work at Harvard; beginning at a new place was always time-consuming.

Beyond this, however, Kate noticed, pulling open the

desk drawers, there were few signs of any work under-
way. Scholars, particularly one of Janet's productivity,
are bound to be in the midst of something. Could Janet
have been murdered for her scholarly work, to be
passed off as the murderer's own? It seemed an improb-
able motive, but it was the first sign yet of a motive
which did not involve Moon or Luellen, and Kate made
careful note of it. Of what, after all, was Howard Falkland not capable?

There was no mail since Janet's death; presumably, it
had been sent on to her family after being vetted for
clues. Kate asked Bill, who confirmed this. He had
turned grumpy, and needed attention. Had there, Kate
asked him, been many condolence notes?

"Yes," Bill said, glad to talk again, "there had."
They had had cards printed up, very handsome, and his
wife Betty had addressed most of them. They had said:
"The family of Janet Needham Mandelbaum wish to
express their profound appreciation for your condol-
ences," or something like that. Kate shuddered, she
hoped unnoticeably. Abhorrer of printed messages, she
tried to defend the practice as necessary in times when
numerous letters had to be answered.

"How many letters?" Kate asked, "just as a guess."
"Oh, many," Bill said. "Fifty, maybe. That's what
Betty said, but she's not very good at counting." Some
of them had come to Bill, sympathy at losing his sister
in so frightful a way. But those that were directed only
at Janet's family came from friends and other professors and ex-students. They had wanted to write to
someone, Kate guessed, and didn't know who. There
must have been many others, she thought, who feeling
grief or loss at Janet's death, had no idea to whom to
write. It would certainly not have occurred to Kate herself to write to Janet's family, whom she had rarely
mentioned.

"Her will left everything to her nieces and nephews, I
understand," Kate said.

"That's right." Bill was clearly annoyed by this. "I

just don't believe in skipping generations," he growled.
"Nick said she didn't like her brothers, and I guess we
gave her a hard time when we were kids. At least she
knew that blood was thicker than water. Money ought
not to be left away from families."

"What is water?" Kate asked.

"Huh?" Bill looked worried, even scared.

"The water that blood is thicker than? What is it,
that water?"

"Well, it's, it's—water. It means you're connected to
people by blood."

"Are people *not* in families connected to people by
water?"

"I suppose that's the sort of darn-fool thing professors ask," Bill said. "Everyone just knows what the
phrase means."

"Sorry," Kate said. "I've always wondered. On to the
bedroom," she added, leaving Bill staring after her, she
hoped not in contemplation of violence.

The police had taken the bed apart and it had not
been remade, for which Kate was grateful. Bill seemed
likely to be given to jokes about beds. The search of the
bed had revealed nothing. Neither had the medicine
cabinet. It contained, in addition to the usual items, a
bottle of phenobarbital, almost full; a prescription had
recently been filled. The bedroom, apart from the bed,
had not been disturbed; Kate's conundrum had clearly
subdued Bill, who probably feared intellectual women.
He stood by her sullenly, exuding impatience.

There was a book on the bed table; only one. Again,
the absence of casual reading puzzled Kate. One would
have expected, if not any recent novels, science fiction
or volumes of culture analysis so popular at this time, at
least a book of criticism or literary theory. The only
book in the room looked new; Kate picked it up from
the night table. It was a text, a Norton Critical Edition
entitled *George Herbert and the Seventeenth Century
Religious Poets*. For some reason, Janet had only recently received it, though the date in the book, Kate

saw, was 1978. Perhaps she was considering it as a text. Kate flipped the pages with her thumb, and the book fell open at page 69. The binding had been slightly forced here, so that the book, opened to this page, lay flat. There was only one poem complete on the page, entitled "Love (III)."[1] The raised number referred to a footnote and Kate lowered her eyes to the bottom of the page, aware of Bill, who was in danger of exploding. The footnote was a biblical quotation: "Blessed are those servants, whom the lord when he cometh shall find watching: verily I say unto you, that he shall gird himself, and make them to sit down to meat, and will come forth and serve them. (Luke 13:37)." Kate returned her glance upward to the poem which she had certainly read before; the (III) presumably meant that Herbert had written three versions of the poem.

Love bade me welcome; yet my soul drew back,
Guilty of dust and sin.
But quick-eyed Love, observing me grow slack
From my first entrance in,
Drew nearer to me, sweetly questioning
If I lacked anything.

"A guest," I answered, "worthy to be here."
Love said, "You shall be he."
"I, the unkind, ungrateful? Ah, my dear,
I cannot look on Thee."
Love took my hand, and smiling, did reply,
"Who made the eyes, but I?"

"Truth, Lord, but I have marred them; let my shame
Go where it doth deserve."
"And know you not," says Love, "who bore the blame?"
"My dear, then I will serve."
"You must sit down," says Love, "and taste my meat."
So I did sit and eat.

"What the blazes are you looking at?" Bill finally asked.

"A poem," Kate said. "By a poet Janet taught very often. Would you like to read it?"

Bill glanced at it. "I can't tell what it's about," he said. "I don't know how to read poetry."

"It was written over three hundred years ago," Kate said.

"Why bother with it, then? Now, I mean. What can it have to do with Janet now?"

"I'm sorry to be holding you up," Kate said. "Do you want to start packing in the kitchen or the living room? I'll only be a moment more." But Bill had no intention of moving from her side.

"Do you want to go through her bureau drawers?" he asked. "That's probably where the jewelry is."

"You look this time," Kate said, "and I'll peer over your shoulder." Bill, glad to have something to do, attacked the bureau drawers with a good deal of vigor. Kate watched for a time.

"Do you mind if I take this book?" she asked Bill, as he retrieved Janet's jewelry box. "I'd like a memento of Janet; I'll be glad to pay you what it costs. The estate belongs to your family, and you should be paid for it, but I don't think you'll miss the book itself."

"All right," Bill said, after a long pause. "There's nothing written in it, is there?" he added, suspicion rising. "Nothing personal?"

"Not that I can see," Kate said. "You look."

Bill took the book, but could find nothing marked in it. He handed it back to Kate with a nod. Kate wrote a check for the price of the book plus a little (the prices of books rise with alarming rapidity) and handed it over with thanks. "Thank you for letting me look," Kate said. "Thank you for behaving so generously."

"Not at all," Bill beamed, now that they were parting. She had not turned out to be a woman worth dawdling over. "Stop in and see us, if you're ever in the Middle West. Take care now." His heartiness returned with his farewell.

Kate, his meaningless phrases echoing in her mind, fled down the stairs and out of Janet's temporary home.

Kate thought she could understand why Janet, with such brothers, would grow up preferring a more formal relationship to men. Bill, Kate had to admit, was enough to put a woman off sex forever.

Chapter 11

A male bastion for more than three centuries, growing over time from a denominational men's college to a major university, Harvard has been slow to recognize changes in ideas about sex roles.
REPORT OF THE COMMITTEE ON THE STATUS OF WOMEN IN THE FACULTY OF ARTS AND SCIENCES

"I ASKED YOU to come and see me, Kate," John Cunningham said the next day, "because those detectives you urged me to hire have found some evidence. Completely negative," he added quickly as Kate looked up, "but with some significance." Kate gazed at him expectantly.

"I hope," he said, "you're going to think it's worth the money. Anyway, they're a good firm. One of the operators we used, believe it or not, used to be a professor of philosophy, complete with Ph.D. He decided to live instead of thinking about life, he said. I figured he'd know something about questions at a university and so did he, so he went on the job. I told Harvard what he was doing, by the way. We don't want more trouble or annoyance than we absolutely need, after all."

"And Harvard didn't object, I take it."

"Let's say I put it to them properly. Let's say, in addition, that I'm a prominent graduate of their law school, and a generous contributor, as well as past and, I may say, markedly successful chairman of our twenty-fifth reunion gift."

"And you made *Law Review* when you were there.

131

Tell me," Kate asked, "suppose you'd been in the bottom half of your law class, which means of course a fractional score lower than the best, and had gone into public interest law, let us say defending women in jail, and never made much money and never contributed more than ten dollars a year, if that. Suppose one of the women in jail had been accused as Moon had been, and you were defending her. Would you have got permission or, anyway, acquiescence?"

"The trouble with you, Kate, is that you're a guilty rich woman who, if you'd gone to Harvard Law School, would have made *Law Review* and contributed plenty. Do you want to hear this evidence or not?"

"Sorry, John. I'm not feeling absolutely tophole, as the English would say."

"Why on earth would they say that? Don't tell me. It happens, to get back to this case on which we are both so feverishly engaged, that on the night in question, the night before Janet Mandelbaum's body was found in the men's room at Warren House, a large number of freshmen in the Yard decided to stay up all night celebrating life. Well, I don't remember what they were celebrating, does it matter? Anyway, they began inside Weld and a few other houses, and what with one thing and another, ended up wandering around in the Yard, and a few of them decided to get air and mildly stoned sitting under the trees. The only point that matters is: there were a great many of these kids all over, and stoned and potted and drunk as they were, the detective thinks it's impossible that they wouldn't have noticed someone carrying someone from anywhere to Warren House. Now just a minute," Cunningham said, raising an admonishing hand, "I know what you're going to say because I said it. Considering what they do in public, and the state they were in, and the fact that absolutely no behavior is considered odd anywhere, at any time, how on earth would they notice? Well, I'll tell you."

"Do," Kate said.

"It so happens there were two women students actually sitting on the steps of Warren House. Finding them was partly luck and partly skill, mostly skill if you ask me. O.K. It occurred to your bright and highly educated detective to see if there had been any complaints that night. And there were, repeated complaints, from two young women living in Weld. Now these two are actually rather interesting because they popped out of the computer together right from the beginning. Don't interrupt. Harvard pairs entering students as roommates by asking them to fill out requirements: can't stand smoking, play only punk rock, that sort of thing. Sounds a nightmare, doesn't it, but thank God it's not our problem. Anyway, these two girls had the only forms that said: must have QUIET, HATE ROCK music and noise, want to work in peace, etc., so of course the computer popped them out as roommates, and they soon became famous as the pair who were always asking for quiet in Weld. I can't decide if they're the only sane pair in the place or if they should have gone to a convent, but that's neither here nor there."

"Oh, I don't know," Kate said. "It seems to me very here about life today. When I went to college, which God knows was an awful experience, at least one spent one's nights in silence. I've walked around Harvard at all hours, believe me, and there is always loud music and raucous noise coming out of the windows. Sometimes the kids play their records as loud as possible *out* the window. Those two may seem like prigs, but I don't know why silence is no longer anyone's right. I'm sure you don't want to hear me on transistor radios on the streets of New York. I mentioned all this to my niece Leighton, and she said people who want quiet should get ear plugs. I thought it more seemly not to continue the discussion."

"Unusual for you," Cunningham said. "Anyway, these two, apparently giving up sleep as a bad job, went over to the Union to play pool—they really are a remarkable pair, I'll give them that—and ended up spending the night on the porch of Warren House, talking. They swear that they mostly contemplated human destiny and hardly dozed at all. They insist no one could have entered Warren House, let alone carrying a body, without their noticing. They were there until the traffic became noticeable, and there were a lot of people about, so our detective thinks the body wasn't moved in the night. It's not conclusive, but it's certainly suggestive."

"Of what?" Kate asked.

"Really, Kate, what's happened to you? You used to be quicker on the uptake. Of the likelihood that she died in Warren House, of course. Clarkville found her body in the morning, quite early. My detective chap says: go yourself and try to act as though you're moving a body. Take a car, go by the streets, go through the Yard, enter from Quincy Street, or Prescott. No one would dare to try it. He swears in any case that no one did. That means that Janet Mandelbaum walked to Warren House and died there. Not that that solves much," Cunningham added, "since any number of people have keys. But it is suggestive, Kate, mighty suggestive."

"Looks bad for the English Department."

"You said it, I didn't," Cunningham concluded.

Again, Kate called from a phone booth in the lobby. Clarkville was in his office, having just finished a department meeting. Yes, he would be glad to see Kate, and would wait for her in the old living room. Kate, emerging some time later from the subway in Harvard Square, made her way to Warren House, thinking of the two girls who had spent the night on its porch. Prigs they might be, but the silence of prigs was less hard on others than the noise of preps. I must try that on Leighton, Kate thought, as she entered Warren House and climbed the stairs.

For the first time Kate took Clarkville in, not as an upset discoverer of a body, not as a sleeping walrus at a Harvard literary society (where after all the paper had been dreadfully dull), not as a reputedly brilliant lecturer on the Victorian novel, but as a large man with a great deal of controlled power and visible charm. Kate was faced with that sudden revelation of someone in all his humanness which often follows one's sense of people as specters, ghouls.

"A dreadful business," Clarkville said. "Dreadful. I don't suppose you've made any progress in deciding what really happened to her?"

"Some," Kate said. "I hope you don't too much resent my part in all this. They've arrested someone and I'm fairly sure he didn't do it."

"I did call you on the morning when I found her body," Clarkville answered. "That certainly gives you some natural interest in the matter."

"And then you know," Kate went on, "her death does reflect so directly on women professors generally that it's not wholly inappropriate for a woman professor to take some part in discovering what happened. My sense, Professor Clarkville, is that you don't like women professors. Is that true? Please don't think I am suggesting that, because you don't like women professors, you would consider murdering one, even in your own department. I hope you see that I see how foolish an idea that is. All the same, perhaps you wouldn't mind telling me your objections to women professors at Harvard."

"I suspect that my horror at the phenomenon of women professors has been greatly exaggerated," Clarkville said. "I won't try to persuade you that I wouldn't have been happier if the whole dreadful subject, forgive me, hadn't come up. But there are many more worried about the whole business than I am, or was. In fact, I thought Janet quite the best seventeenth-century person we could get, particularly if we didn't want to be flooded with the latest in semiology and deconstructionism, and frankly I was rather more amused than not. Oh, given a choice, I'd have chosen not to have a woman professor in the department. It's bound to cause problems, just in the nature of things. But I haven't become as dead set against women professors as some have. Most of our best students are women; that's true everywhere in graduate studies at the moment, so it seems only right that they should have at least one representative of their sex on the faculty of the department. And then, of course, I *was* glad that Janet wasn't a real feminist, always being offended if one held the door for her." He smiled.

"I don't think any woman feels offended at that." Kate smiled back. "It's always the stupidest men, quite frankly, who make jokes about that, hold the door for you and then say coyly that they hope they're not being male chauvinist pigs in doing it. Such a bore. Do you find me particularly difficult to talk to? If you do, say so, and I'll spare you my theories." In fact, Kate found that Clarkville's humanness wore thin under scrutiny.

"I don't find you difficult to deal with, no. I might if you insisted on defending women's studies courses."

"In which you don't believe."

"I don't really think there is such a thing. I teach George Eliot, as you know. If there is some other approach to her, or to other women novelists, I would hope to be able to embrace it in a general way, without labeling the course 'women's studies.' "

"There you are then," Kate said. "You would be shifting your emphasis because of feminism; that's all women's studies are about, just as you have doubtless shifted some emphasis because of Marx and Freud and Einstein. Even Samuel Johnson is now seen benignly in a Freudian light."

"Well, you put it reasonably. I dare say I'm prejudiced. It seems faddish. Did you want to see me to discuss George Eliot and feminism, because if you did, I'm willing." Clarkville shifted in his chair. "I just want to know the agenda."

"What I really wanted to discuss," Kate said, "was a theory."

"A literary theory?" Did Kate catch a note of hope in his voice?

"No. A theory about Janet's body. I think it was in Warren House that she died. I don't think her body was brought here, because it would have been almost impossible for that to be done without anyone seeing it.

Besides, why should someone bring her here if she had died somewhere else?"

"I see what you mean," Clarkville said. "How can I help you?"

"First of all, by telling me frankly and without leaving anything out what happened here the evening before Janet died. Let me induce you to be frank not only by the many references I might offer to my fine nature and upstanding principles, but also by using a little benevolent blackmail. Things have been pretty easy on the Harvard English Department up to now. You are, in fact, the only tenured member of it I have met. But if we don't find out the truth about this, I can promise you that the department and all its members are going to be very much involved. On the other hand, if we can get at the truth and discover what did happen, it's sure to be a whole lot less embarrassing for everyone. We might even avoid putting some of the faculty through prolonged and annoying questioning."

"Is there some reason why you think I may be willing to tell you what happened the evening before she died, or able to tell you?"

"Let's just say for the moment that since you shared the discovery of the body with me," Kate said, "you might want me to share this theory with you."

"The trouble is, you know," Clarkville said, getting up and beginning to lumber about the room, "that one truth leads, so to speak, to another which, however true, one might wish to conceal. If you see what I mean."

"I do see, but we disagree on the implied strategy. A few people with knowledge are better at concealing certain facts than more people with no knowledge blundering about; and they *will* come blundering about, Professor Clarkville, that I can promise you. And of course I shall tell them all I know or guess."

"Which you haven't done yet."

"Not yet. Let's begin with that afternoon. It hasn't occurred to any of us to think about that. What happened the afternoon before her death?"

"We had a department meeting."

"Here?"

"Yes. Down the hall, where we always hold them. It went on for a bit; not the whole department, just the tenured professors, including Janet of course."

"Did anything happen at the meeting that you think—I don't want to put words into your mouth?"

"We discussed possible hirings, and promotions. That's mostly what tenured professors here, meeting as a body, discuss; it's no doubt the same where you are. We have to hire some assistant professors for next year, we talked about what fields we needed them in, and the chairman mentioned that we had had another petition for some women's studies courses in the English Department. Our chairman is not exactly amenable to the idea of women's studies and, as I've suggested to you, most of us think it is a fad and will pass, but the fact is Harvard has started a women's studies program and the English Department can scarcely refuse to have anything to do with it. Our policy, the chairman explained, was to let anyone who wanted to teach such a course teach it. Someone suggested that we hire a young woman assistant professor who might want to teach something, and another man, one of the more, ah, forward-looking of our professors in this respect said why should the courses always be taught by assistant professors. One of the problems with the program in our department is that no tenured women or men, of course, teach them. Well, everyone looked more or less inquiringly at Janet."

Clarkville paused and Kate waited for him to go on. His demeanor suggested he had not finished speaking, but he did not speak. "Yes?" Kate finally said.

"She, well, she—" it was clear Clarkville was searching for the politic phrase—"she rather flew off the handle, don't you know. Got a bit upset. Said why should she be saddled with that, she was a seventeenth-century scholar, if there was a woman's point of view on Donne and Marvell and Milton she didn't know what it was, and so on, and so forth. You can imagine it, I'm sure.

In short, she considered the whole suggestion preposterous." Clarkville paused again. "Well," he went on, "that was a bit embarrassing, of course, we're not exactly used to scenes, at least not of that sort—the fact is the whole thing might have passed over had we gone on to something else, but alas, one of our members—let me be allowed at least for the moment not to name him—said, 'Since it is only the efforts of those women's studies devotees who have brought you here, Professor Mandelbaum, I can't imagine why you want to take so high and mighty a tone. Of course women's studies are nonsense, pure nonsense. So is affirmative action. So is most of what goes on in the world today, with governments running universities and everything else besides. But since we've got saddled with you, it does seem the least you could do would be to take care of this problem for us.'"

Kate stared at Clarkville. "As a young reporter I have recently met would say, Wow."

"Yes," Clarkville went on. "Naturally we were all upset at his saying this. He is given to rather extreme conservative opinions—I am sorry, something cannot be rather extreme, I'm afraid I'm feeling the strain—and tact is not his long suit. What he said was not only tactless, it was not even true. After all, we had all confirmed the search committee's choice of a woman professor who was perfectly safe on the subject of feminism and women's studies. Perhaps that was a mistake, as I look back on it now. While we were all remonstrating with this chap, Janet began to cry. Very quietly, you know, and it was clear she absolutely couldn't help herself and would have given anything not to be crying. Women are so aware that men do not cry at public meetings. I'm afraid it was all rather . . ."

"Embarrassing," Kate offered.

"Yes, it was. We none of us quite knew what to do, and we rather waited, don't you know, for her to leave the room. But she didn't. She just sat there with the tears running down her face. Finally, the chairman suggested that perhaps we had better adjourn the meeting, and we did. Rather abruptly, I'm afraid. She still sat there and one by one we left. I did think of staying, you know, of offering some sort of sympathy, but it was hard to know what was wanted. And that," Clarkville concluded, "is the last time any of us saw her alive. Except, of course, for the murderer, as one is supposed ominously to add."

"And none of this has been told to the police?"

"The police were rather minimal in their questions to us. And it did seem least said, soonest mended, as my dear mother used to say. If it's any comfort to you, I do think we all behaved badly; very badly indeed. But we aren't used to dealing with women as colleagues, and to tell you the truth she was the last woman I would have thought would have done anything like that, crying at a meeting, don't you know."

They sat together for a time in silence. Then Kate spoke: "Professor Clarkville, that may have been the last time you saw her alive, but it wasn't the last time you saw her, was it? I mean, aside from finding her body in the men's room."

"Meaning?" Clarkville said.

"Meaning that I think, I *know*—the secretaries know—that you went into the chairman's office that morning. I think you found her there." There was a long silence.

"How did you know?" Clarkville at last asked.

"An educated guess. The men's room never seemed very logical, for all its jocular possibilities as an indication that women were out of place here. But we know the body was moved after death, in fact after rigor had begun or was fully in effect, if that's the right phrase. Rigor begins soon after death and is gone in twenty-four hours; I've managed to learn that much, though I'm sure there's plenty of room for mistakes. Why would someone move the body to the men's room? Not an illogical place, after all. My guess that the body was in a position with the legs drawn up: the death is a painful and convulsive one; putting the body on the toilet in the stall may have seemed, under the circum-

stances, the logical thing. Then, to have left it in the
chairman's office would have incriminated him. Finally, why do I think *you* found her in that office?
Again, a guess. The simplest explanation usually makes
the most sense. You found her, you moved her, you
'discovered' the body. As to why she died in the chairman's office, I don't know that. I assume that you
didn't kill her. Why do I assume that? Because you are
a highly intelligent man, and you are unlikely to have
killed her in that office, or at all. But you were disturbed after moving her, and you called me as well as
the police to have someone who would be upset to try
the story on. That wasn't the height of kindness, was it,
or gallantry, if you prefer?"

"I knew she was dead," Clarkville said. "As you say,
the body had stiffened into a more or less sitting position. My first thought was to get her out of there. I did
think of the ladies' room again, to make it all seem part
of some plot, I wouldn't have had to carry the body
downstairs if I'd left it in the ladies' room, but I
couldn't do that to the secretaries; the stall in the men's
room seemed better. I called you, believe it or not, because I thought I wanted someone here who cared for
her. I couldn't think of anyone else, and I'd heard you
were friends." But it was clear that Clarkville's tone of
quiet reasonableness hid fear.

"More or less," Kate said. "More or less."

"I hope you do believe I didn't kill her."

Kate ignored this. "Whoever killed her," she said,
"was with her in that office, and forced or persuaded
her to take the cyanide in a drink. He removed all the
evidence when he left. Only for Sherlock Holmes do
murderers leave bits of tobacco behind. You didn't
clear anything away, apart from the body?"

"Heavens no, except for her handbag, which I left
with the body. My only thought, and I recognize it
wasn't a particularly commendable one, was to get her
out of there. I thought, frankly, though I see how little
credit it does me, that if her body was found in there
we'd never hear the end of it. The men's room seemed

more general territory. It is interesting, however," Clarkville mused now, almost in a scholarly way, "how fast and calmly one's mind works in an emergency."

"I take it," Kate said, "that as in my university, one key fits all the doors?"

"Yes," Clarkville said. "We have talked about changing that; thefts, you know, and pilferage."

"Will you do something for me?" Kate asked.

"If I can. Are you going to the police with this story?"

"Not until I have to. What I want is to see Janet's office. I know the police have just released it for department use. Could I have a look before anyone gets ready to clean it out?"

"Of course," Clarkville said, rising to his feet. "Her office is in Widener. They'll let you in over there. I'll wait for you here, if you don't mind. When you're finished, stop for me and we'll leave together. I'd like to hear what you found, and walk part of the way with you. Silly, no doubt, but I cannot contemplate another woman professor of whatever university meeting a problem here of any kind."

"Thank you," Kate said, taking the keys. She stood there for a moment, her eyes meeting Clarkville's. It was perfectly possible that this was a trap, that he was a maniac and a murderer, but Kate doubted it. She decided to take her chances. Clarkville stepped outside into the hall and switched on a light so that she could see her way to the stairs, and out; she passed the famous ladies' room, where it all began, Kate thought as she left.

Janet's office, rather unexpectedly, looked more used, more lived-in, than her apartment. Here some books she might have been reading for pleasure lay strewn about. She must have spent a good deal of time in her office, waiting, perhaps, or working. Kate sat in Janet's desk chair and looked around her. One of the books Janet had been reading, which lay on the desk, was Volume II of the life of Eleanor Marx, by Yvonne Kapp. Other biographies and recent books lay in piles around the room; only this volume was on the desk. It was not a biography Kate would, offhand, have connected with Janet. Nor, for that matter, would Kate have guessed that Janet would do her nonscholarly reading here. Was this office a home away from home, a place where news might come, where something welcome might happen? Reining in her fancies, Kate concluded merely that Janet worked more here, committed herself more.

When Kate returned to Warren House Clarkville was waiting where she had left him. "I've taken a book from her office," Kate said. "Do you think anyone will mind? I've already bought one of Janet's books, also a paperback, from the estate, and am ready to buy another. I thought I would read it to see what interested Janet in Eleanor Marx."

"Take it by all means," Clarkville said. "I don't know much about Eleanor Marx, except that she translated *Madame Bovary*. That's still the translation many of my students use. I certainly can't think of anyone less likely to interest Janet. How little we know of each other."

"How much, now that you mention it, do you know of Howard Falkland?" Kate asked. "Is he a particular student of yours?"

"Meaning what?" Clarkville inquired with some asperity.

"Meaning," Kate said, meeting his eyes, "would he have put strong vodka into the drink of someone unused to much alcohol because you had suggested that would be a clever thing to do?"

Clarkville stared at Kate for a perceptible minute. Then he switched out the lights and ushered her out of the front door and on to the porch.

"Howard Falkland," Clarkville said as they descended the stairs, "is a fool."

Chapter 12

> [*It is easier*] *to quell emotion than to incur the consequences of venting it.*
> GEORGE ELIOT
> *Middlemarch*

KATE SPENT the next day locked up in her study at the Institute. She was reading, mainly, and thinking, and pacing about on the small floor. For a time in the middle of the day she walked around Cambridge again. But the streets, now that winter was ending, were too crowded; one could scarcely make one's way up Brattle Street, even single file. Kate gave it up, and settled back with her books: a novel, two biographies, and the textbook from Janet's apartment containing Herbert's poems. Kate had sent off a check to Bill for Volume II of the biography of Eleanor Marx. No doubt the in-laws had taken no thought of Janet's office. But Kate was scrupulous in money matters, not to say fastidious: she might lend a large sum of money in no expectation of seeing it again, but disliked not having a small loan repaid. This was the sort of thing, she knew, which made her so straight in the eyes of the women in the coffee house on Hampshire Street.

Kate had by now memorized Herbert's poem "Love," and had read through the entire selection of Herbert's poems in the book to see if any other poem seemed to have been studied by Janet. But only "Love," it seemed, had been so carefully perused. It was only now, as Kate flipped the pages back and forth, that she saw what her eye had missed many times before: a small addition in Janet's neat hand. Under the last Herbert poem whose title was printed on page viii of the table of contents, another title had been written in: "Hope." There was, of course, no page given, since the poem was not included in the text. Kate had missed the addition before because Janet had printed it so neatly in letters that approximated type.

Kate left the study once again and made her way out of the Radcliffe Yard onto Garden Street, up Garden Street to Shepherd Street and the Hilles Library, almost running. Kate liked the Hilles Library which, except in exam and reading periods, was rarely much occupied. It lacked the thick ambience of undergraduate passion and derision which filled Lamont, the undergraduate library in Harvard Yard. She by now knew her way around Hilles, and ran up the modern wooden stairs to the floor housing English literature. She wanted any collection of Herbert's poems, ancient or modern. There were many, and it did not take Kate long to discover that Herbert had indeed written a poem entitled "Hope," and that it was short:

> *I gave to Hope a watch of mine: but he*
> > *An anchor gave to me.*
> *Then an old prayer-book I did present:*
> > *And he an optick sent.*
> *With that I gave a viall full of tears:*
> > *But he a few green eares.*
> *Ah Loyterer! I'le no more, no more I'le bring!*
> > *I did expect a ring.*

Kate sat down at one of the tables and read the poem over and over. She copied it out onto a piece of paper she borrowed from a student, since she had left her study so precipitously. Then she returned the book of poems to the shelf and went to see if Moon was home. He usually was, in the late afternoon.

Moon offered Kate a beer, and agreed to talk about Janet. "You think you're on to something?" he asked. "I'd like you to get that bail money back; I'd like to find out what I owe Cunningham and maybe borrow to pay him off. I'd like to finish up my class and get the hell out of here. Since it's clear you're the only prayer I've got for any of those things, I'll talk about Janet all you like. But I wish I could see what good it will do. Try to understand, Kate, I haven't seen the woman in nearly twenty years. The clue to why she was killed, and who wanted to kill her, isn't likely to lie in my rather tarnished memories. To be frank, they weren't exactly glistening ten minutes after the divorce."

"What did you think of her family? I've just met a brother, an experience not to be repeated."

"Thought wasn't something I bothered wasting on her family, and I honestly don't think Janet did either. She had those two younger brothers who must have been competing for an award as the dullest member of the local Elks Club. Oh, I don't mean that to sound as snobbish as I'm sure it does; I'm trying to suggest that if you had a club whose qualifications for initiation were being as conventional and macho as possible, her brothers would have been founding members."

"You and Janet didn't quarrel about that?"

"Never. I agreed to the church wedding, since the idea of her marrying a Jew was hard enough for them to swallow, but she was perfectly clear she was going through the church wedding as a final gesture toward their ideas. Janet didn't let go of convictions easily, God knows, but I think she had managed to separate her fantasies about her childhood from the facts by the time we got married; in fact, that's probably *why* we got married."

"Had she had a happy childhood, did you gather?"

"Not a bit happy. But she always had the sense that something from that childhood was going to be redeemed, acted out—I don't know what the word I want is—she was going to show them when she grew up. The trouble with that is, you show them, you become the smartest girl in college and graduate school, and all they can say is, When are you going to get married? I don't think Janet wanted to get married, but she wasn't going to let them think she couldn't. But she also wasn't going to marry one of their kind. I guess I fitted the bill, particularly since I'd been after her persistently to marry me and get the hell into bed with me. Christ, how I hate the fifties."

"Moon," Kate said, after a long pause in which they both remembered the fifties without pleasure, "if you were to choose on the basis of what you know about Janet, whether someone murdered her through personal hatred of her as a person, or because of what she stood for, which would it be?"

"Would she have been murdered for being Janet, or for being Janet's sort of person? Is that the question? On the basis of my knowledge of her, the latter every time. I don't for a moment believe she was murdered because she had offended someone, however deeply. She was murdered because of what she was and where she was and what she represented. Which explains, of course, why I didn't do it, as you have already figured out and will soon prove."

"I know you hate Henry James, Moon, but you embody one of the qualities his favorite hero, Strether in *The Ambassadors,* most admired: the unattainable art of taking things as they come."

"I don't say James wasn't insightful, only too long-winded and complicated in his syntax for my tastes. I do take things as they come, but Janet never could. Do you know what she really wanted? She wanted to be a collaborator with destiny. She wanted to fill some marvelous role that had been set out for her by God Almighty, or the equivalent. Of course no one collaborates with destiny; destiny, if we really know what we want, sometimes collaborates with us. She liked the seventeenth century where God appeared and said, Trust me, my child, or words to that effect."

"Moon, did you ever tell her how you felt in the war?"

"Oh, yes. Some of our best times together were talking about how we'd felt when young. Those were the times we understood each other best, I think, when we were closest. She never liked sex that much, which I may have mentioned, but she liked to talk sometimes, she liked to be held while she remembered. It probably did me more good to talk to her than it did her to talk to me, if you want to know the truth."

"There's only one question left to ask, Moon. Think carefully before you answer it; very carefully." And she asked him.

So in the end Kate went off to Boston to lay it all before John Cunningham. They had agreed some days before to call off the detectives; they had done their job well, but the results were all negative. Kate had observed to John that the trouble with the universe—"My God, spare me," Cunningham had groaned—was that negativity was insufficiently applauded, rewarded, understood. "We all cheer when someone *does* something," Kate had said, "even if it turns out later to be what Leighton calls an asshole thing to have done. But who cheers when someone avoids something? No cheers, no credit, no applause." Cunningham had answered that he wished to God Kate would not get him into these conversations during his office hours. "You're worse than my wife," he had said, "explaining to me some demand of the children's which is idiotic, but she means to wear me out so that I'll say yes."

On this occasion, Cunningham had agreed to meet after office hours; what's more, he had agreed to take her to dinner at Locke-Ober's, a restaurant he accused her of liking because, like Harvard, it used not to let women into most of its sacred precincts. Kate denied this, saying what she liked was the creamed spinach and the courtly manner of the older waiters who tended to be deaf and placating.

"I only consented to this restaurant," Cunningham assured her when they were seated, "because the dinner is so large and will take us so long to eat that you will have time to finish what I am sure is going to be a preposterous story. Mr. Mandelbaum's case comes up the week after next, by the way. I hope he isn't going to jump bail, leaving me to explain to Reed why, when he married you for your money—I mean what other attractions could there be, you talk too much and were already aging at the time—I allowed you to blow the lot on bail and lost it."

"I promise you Moon will not run off to Pago Pago."

"I promise you he won't too. Even Moon must know that Pago Pago is an American possession, and that he would be retrievable. I don't understand why people spend fortunes, absolute fortunes these days, educating girls who end up not knowing the most elementary geography. What will you drink?"

"Just for that," Kate said examining the wine list, "I'm going to have a bottle of Vouvray, Clos de Nouys, 1971. I know it says demi-sec, but it happens to have been a lovely wine that year, and I branch out from absolutely dry wines from time to time, when inspired."

"Very well. Have a Scotch first. Two Scotches," he said to the waiter, "you know the brand, and stick that wine in a cooler for us. In fact, you better put two bottles aside, I have a distinct premonition we are going to be here for a long time."

"John, I know you don't like professional women like me, but aren't you acting a bit of a bully, even for you? Is something the matter?"

"Of course something's the matter. You're about to tell me that one of the most distinguished professors at Harvard has killed a female colleague because he couldn't stand the thought of women in his department in the higher ranks. I'm going to take on the whole damn Harvard administration. I'm going to have to fight about that damn chair they got endowed with by some half-besotted lunatic if you want my opinion. And the fact that the professor is queer is going to come out, and we are going to get expert witnesses arguing about whether homosexuality is or isn't likely to lead to the murder of women, and you ask me if something is the matter."

"You think Clarkville did it, then?"

"No. I think you think Clarkville did it. You said on the phone she died in the chairman's office."

"That's right. She did. And Clarkville moved the body. I don't doubt for a moment he would have liked to kill her, at least from time to time, but he didn't do it. He didn't have the opportunity, or the means, to take your sine qua non, and he didn't even have mine: the motive. Because if there was one thing Clarkville was smart enough to figure out it's that the last thing his department wanted was publicity about a female professor. Any publicity, except perhaps that she had joined the Total Woman movement and had taken to the road to preach female subservience and bound feet."

"My God, what a relief. You don't think Clarkville did it. Not some other Harvard professor, then, dear Kate; you haven't let me off one frightful prospect to face me with another equally bad?"

"Well, I have to admit she was killed by a Harvard professor of English; there is, in fact, only one Harvard English professor it could have been."

"Yes?" Cunningham asked, keeping his eyes on Kate while beckoning frantically for the waiter and another Scotch. "Yes?"

"Janet herself," Kate said. "Opportunity, means, motive. And a little help from everybody, everybody at Harvard, that is, and one rather distinguished poet, dead himself, named Herbert."

By the time they got around to the Vouvray, Cunningham was beginning to look as though tomorrow might just be marginally worth staying sober for. "Tell me," he said, "tell me. I'll buy you two dinners, and five bottles of anything they've got if you can convince me of this one."

"To start at the beginning," Kate said (John groaned pitifully; Kate ignored him), "why hit on Moon as the murderer? I know he is the most unlikely type to kill anyone, let alone poor Janet, but that can't have been motive enough even for the Boston police. Then, of course, they turned to poor Luellen May. What confused us all was that so many people got involved in this who had nothing to do with it. I mean, here Moon and I were from her past, but our being here seemed to have more connection with Janet than it actually had. Moon's being here was pure coincidence, but they could scarcely believe *that* when, in addition, he possessed cyanide. Luellen May had been found with Janet in that bathtub. I, ignoring the past, recent or ancient, suspected Clarkville, or somebody working at his behest. Don't you like the word 'behest'? It's the residue of a childhood spent reading the proper books. All right, all right. I suspected Howard Falkland as an instrument of Clarkville's, and even other unnamed professors who had been lying low."

"Kate, you better have some proof of this, because it's already beginning to sound like one of those stories the police don't find particularly funny, even in their lighter moments."

"Be patient, dear boy, be patient. Where was I? Oh, yes, my suspects. First of all, we had the incident in the bathtub. Now Howard Falkland behaved like the true idiot he is, but he wasn't criminal within the meaning of the act. He poured some hundredproof vodka into the drink of a woman who was not used to alcohol . . ."

"Unlike some others I might mention."

"If careless persiflage is what you're looking for, I'm ready to oblige."

"I beg your pardon; humbly, I recall my words. Go on, my good woman, go on."

"He probably overdid it. She didn't taste it of course, not in Campari. And what he didn't know is that she had been taking whopping doses of phenobarbital. She didn't believe in tranquilizers, but she allowed herself a perfectly honest old-fashioned drug with the same effect, much cheaper, and quite commonly used when she was young."

"Why *does* everyone take tranquilizers these days?"

"When you have the time, I'll explain the drug industry to you. In addition, it's fatal to take an overdose of phenobarbital. Overdoses on tranquilizers are harder to achieve."

"Then why didn't she simply take too many of her pills and leave us all a quiet note? Why the chairman's office and cyanide?"

"Don't try to rush me. I'm still working it out in my own mind. You don't have to hear it, of course."

"What makes you think I had a choice, once you called me into the case? Get on with it, get on with it."

"The alcohol, plus a probably larger-than-usual dose of phenobarbital, caused the little episode in the famous mahogany ladies' room at Warren House. Howard then capped his sophomoric efforts by calling a woman he knew was radical, feminist and gay. This frightened Janet badly, put Luellen May in danger, and makes me unwilling to admit that Howard Falkland isn't a murderer after all. I suspect the shock of passing out at a party, and then of finding herself associated with that woman in a police station—or some version of a police station—must have caused Janet terror, and not alone terror, but despair. And of course there was another effect: Janet asked for me. Even I, who was not particularly smart about any of this from start to finish, realized when I first saw Janet how alone she was. She belonged nowhere, poor Janet. And she turned to me for help, and to Sylvia. I'll explain Sylvia in a minute. But instead of telling her she was a hero, a great girl, stick with it and those men will see your sterling qualities, we told her she was standing up for womanhood. Perfectly true, of course, but hardly comforting to one who had wanted to join the male club and who didn't conceive of womanhood as anything worth standing up for, now or ever."

"How did Sylvia, whoever she is, get into all this?"

Kate told him about Sylvia. "Janet got chosen for the hot seat, and Sylvia was enough of a politician to see that a lot of forces would like to ambush this one, and she wanted to do what she could. How many donors of million-dollar chairs for women are there likely to be?

Don't answer that, I dislike you when you become coarse."

"So after the bathtub bit, Janet went from bad to worse."

"I'm afraid so. The whole pattern of despair began to suggest itself when I looked at her apartment: bare, never made into a home, as though she knew it would never be a home, and by her bedside the poems of Herbert. I haven't read seventeenth-century poetry since I stopped teaching the survey of English literature donkey's years ago, but even then we didn't have much time for Herbert, so I came to this poem she was concentrating on with a fresh mind, the way one ought to go to poems, of course. My guess is that in a certain way Janet began to read it for the first time too, letting it strike her. Her early, famous book was about reading Herbert as his contemporaries read him, not as we read him now, but she was reading him now, with passion, I suppose, and receiving the full emotional shock of his poem." Kate stopped to drink some wine.

"The poem of Herbert's, 'Love,' " she went on, "speaks for a man who considers himself unworthy in his life and religion, being urged to sit down with Christ and be served by him. I needn't tell you in how many ways the poem can be read. Relax, I won't tell you. What eventually occurred to me is that it could be read as an invitation to death, that one was ready to join Christ in heaven, to get there, furthermore, by eating. Eating death, perhaps. All right, no objections necessary, I dismissed this fancy as just that: fancy.

"And then," Kate went on, "I remembered something, a rather fuzzy conversation in the dining hall at Dunster when a young man told me he had consulted Janet about a poem of Herbert's that Simone Weil had read. So off I went to read the most recent biography of Simone Weil, looking for hints. What I found was that Simone Weil had copied this poem out in her own hand; she felt, while reading it, that Christ was *there*. Weil, dear John, in case you suspect me of foisting off another feminist on you, was a brilliant philosopher who worked all her life for the poor, the tortured, the betrayed. She identified herself profoundly with poverty, persecution and all suffering, except, of course, the only kinds of suffering she had experienced personally: as a woman, and as a Jew. She didn't particularly identify with either."

"Did she kill herself?"

"Perhaps. She starved to death when many people were starving, during World War II. I think she died in part from not having a proper place in which to suffer. The point to remember is that she had one of the great minds of our time. I hope you've got Weil firmly in place, because I'm about to drag in more dead women, fictional and real, so prepare yourself." But John, a man fundamentally wise, did not josh Kate now.

"After I'd established that Clarkville had moved Janet's body, and all that, I asked him to let me see her office. She had done what living she did at Harvard there: that much was immediately clear. It was there that salvation, if it came, would come. And she was reading a biography of Eleanor Marx."

"It doesn't sound like Janet's sort of subject."

"Just what I thought, and what Clarkville said. But I went away and read the biography. Eleanor Marx killed herself with cyanide, then called prussic acid. No one, with the possible exception of one friend to whom she was writing, even knew she felt depressed. Furthermore," Kate announced, while Cunningham poured her more wine, "Eleanor Marx translated *Madame Bovary,* whose heroine, in despair at having no place to live her life, and no life to live, kills herself by eating arsenic. She said she wanted it for rats; Eleanor Marx said she wanted it for a dog. She was Marx's daughter, by the way."

"Arsenic," Cunningham said. "And yet Janet chose cyanide. Arsenic is much easier to come by."

"True, in the ordinary way. But Janet had cyanide. She had had it many years. She stole it from Moon years ago, when they were married and he told her about it. She only took one capsule, or two. I think she took two in fear that the poison might have weakened over the years."

"Wouldn't sleeping pills be easier, or her phenobarbital?"

"Much easier. There are two important factors about cyanide, which is why the military and spies use it. It is fast, and it is irreversible. There is no turning back, and no one can bring you back."

"Why take it in the chairman's office?"

"I can't explain that; I can only guess. It had to be a gesture toward a man, perhaps even revengeful. The chairman had that day taken away any hope. You see, there was another poem she had been thinking of, another poem of Herbert's, called 'Hope.' This poem suggests that the poet had had hope of returns from Hope, because he had believed in him. It ends with the line: 'Ah Loyterer! I'le no more, no more I'le bring! I did expect a ring.' That seems to say it fairly clearly. Besides," Kate rather offhandedly added, "if she'd died in her own office she might not have been found until the cleaning woman found her, thus underlining what seemed to Janet the real failure of her life: no one would miss her. I haven't told you about the department meeting, and so on. Perhaps that can wait. It only suggests what hell she was in."

"And you asked Moon if she could have stolen the capsules?"

"I did. Moon said he had shown her the capsules. He talked often of death in those days, and the terrible times of the war in the Pacific. I remember that. He even said, with his rare honesty, that it had occurred to him that she might take one or two, but he decided then that anyone had the right to die, and that anyway, Janet was the least likely person to commit suicide, let alone with cyanide. But times change people. And Janet was always a woman of determination. Once she made up her mind to die, she was not to be deterred by anyone. No more than Eleanor Marx, or Emma Bovary or Simone Weil did she mean to be rescued. I like to think she died believing she had been called to a holy feast, but I don't believe it. That kind of faith belonged to Herbert's time, and Herbert's sort. I want to believe she believed, for my own sake."

Chapter 13

---

*That the Faculty endorse the major conclusion of the
Committee on the Status of Women, 'that the number
of women on the Faculty must be increased,' and
urge its officers, its department chairmen, and the
members of its search committees to work toward
that end.*

VOTED AT A REGULAR MEETING
OF THE FACULTY OF ARTS AND
SCIENCES

AND SO, in the end, Kate had half the term left for her
own devices. Mostly she worked on her lecture for the
Institute, to be given in May. Even as she wrote it, she
dedicated it to Janet. Herbert had written:

> *Who would have thought my shrivl'd heart
> Could have recover'd greennesse?*

Even as Kate's heart, like the spring, again brightened,
she mourned that Janet's heart had not recovered
greennesse.

When Kate finally gave the lecture in May, in the
large lecture hall in Agassiz House where these events
were held, she spoke on the new forms possible to
women in making fictions of female destiny. ("I'm not
coming," Moon said, "I refuse to contemplate you
being polysyllabic, structuralist and theoretical"; but he
came.)

"And you," Sylvia asked after the talk, "are you
going to stay on at Harvard to contrive new forms, new

fictions of female destiny?" Again they had their feet up, and were watching the boats and rafts on the river, and the students on the grass at the river's edge.

"I'm staying for Leighton's graduation anyway," Kate said, "though it means meeting my family. Clarkville has sent me a good faculty seat, however, so I shall not have to sit with them. It didn't of course occur to him that I might need more than one, bless his narrow male heart. Anyway, I have high hopes of Leighton."

"Janet was murdered all the same," Sylvia said. She kept looking at the river. "We all conspired in it. We isolated her, we gave her no community. Only death welcomed her."

"I trust," Kate said, "that Harvard at least has some sense of what it has done. You know, in an odd way, we understand this place better than most. Didn't Kipling or someone write, 'He little knows of England who only England knows.' If Harvard males figure that out, she may not have died for nothing."

"She didn't, I'm sure of that. The professors in the Harvard English Department thought they could say the time for worrying about women had passed, that the feminist movement had spent itself in academia. I doubt they'll say that anymore, or choose so badly, the next time."

"So there will be a next time?"

"Oh, yes. The endowed chair's still in place," Sylvia said.

"I am surprised, but by God, I'm pleased. Do you notice I seem to be mentioning God more often. The effect of George Herbert, no doubt."

"No doubt. Janet's death has merely inspired the donor to greater efforts. There may now be two endowed chairs for women. Harvard is going to pay greater attention to *two* million dollars, we can trust their financially astute little hearts for that."

"Am I ever to learn who the donor is?"

"Why not. You deserve to. But you must tell no one, because the one thing that might really scare her off is publicity. She doesn't want to admit an interest in women. She trades in men."

"Whatever can you mean?"

"My dear, she's a wealthy old woman worth millions of dollars, and she owns a baseball team. Did you know someone could own a baseball team? Probably you did, but I didn't. I thought they belonged to cities. Cities have franchises, but people own teams, and almost anybody can own the stadiums."

"What a mountain of information you are. How on earth did you get to this woman, whoever got to her?"

"She got convinced that if she was happily dropping five million a year on a baseball team, she could drop a million or two in one fell swoop on the delightful exercise of annoying Harvard. Isn't it wonderful? I'm told she attends every game her team plays, at home and away. It was whispered that there are three kinds of women in the lives of her players: their wives, the women they sport with on the road, and their owner. She, you'll notice, is the only one in a class by herself."

"What convinced her to give the chairs? She doesn't sound the sort to go in for academic women."

"A lot of people helped. Millionaires know one another, and the Harvard types rallied round. After all, a million dollars is a million dollars, even from a dame. But what seems to have actually done it was a fact that emerged at the meeting I told you about, the one where all the women at Harvard met for the first time. One of the speakers was a black woman who reported that she had not been allowed to live in the dormitories when she first came to Radcliffe because she was black. The most dramatic moment in the baseball woman's life, it turned out, was when Branch Rickey first brought Blacks into baseball. She cheered for Jackie Robinson when the other players were spiking him and the fans were loosing black cats onto the playing field. She understood that kind of prejudice, and I think she would have liked to do something for Blacks at Harvard, but they managed to convince her that Harvard was well aware of the race problem, but still thought women were creatures who ought to lap up learning, paying through the teeth, and shut up. That's what did it—that and a marvelously persuasive black woman I'd like you to meet one day."

"I think," Kate said, "I'll buy a season ticket out of sheer gratitude, and follow her team's batting average. The sort of thing one ought to take up in one's declining years."

Soon after Kate's talk, she and Moon set out to have dinner at the coffee house on Hampshire Street. They had been invited by Joan Theresa, Luellen May and Jocasta. Moon planned to leave soon after, when all the papers had been submitted in his writing course. He declined an invitation to teach the course again next year. "Not even if you were to be here," he said to Kate. She had her bail money back, but Moon had had to give up the capsules. He seemed resigned to that; their need, Kate surmised, had long since passed.

"Luellen asked me to ask you," Moon said to Kate, "if you would testify in court for her, to say she was a responsible person to raise her children. She is, you know. Much more responsible than her husband, who's rather like your Howard Falkland, I'd say."

"Well, at least the police have more or less ungraciously admitted that Luellen had nothing to do with Janet's death, which is more than can be said of the rest of us."

"Kate, Janet's death has been officially declared a suicide, and I suggest you just relax and let it go at that. I don't like the way you're growing maudlin, blaming yourself and adopting other unbecoming attitudes. It's not like you. Can I tell Luellen you'll be a witness to her fine character when she goes to court?"

"I'll testify," Kate said. "We don't want another victim of this mess. But though I would admit it to no one else, I'm a teeny bit tired of pulling Harvard's chestnuts out of the fire, particularly when I'd rather see them all, and especially the English Department, slowly roasting.

And not a word of thanks, of course, or even further notice of one's existence. Promise not to tell anyone I said so."

"Your confidences, like you, are forever safe with me," Moon said. He shifted his guitar, and put his arm around her for a moment. "I shall miss you," he said, and then dropped his arm. "You are all of Harvard that I shall miss. Not my sort of place at all. Good to have found that out once and for all."

The dinner was a fine occasion. Kate had agreed not to smoke in exchange for wine: a fair bargain, Joan Theresa had said, and provided a homemade wine that was, Kate was surprised to discover, not half bad. She had always suspected homemade wine of tasting sugary. "You are not to bring anything," Luellen had said. "This is in your honor, and for your sake Jocasta will be just outside of the window where we sit. You may fling her things, if you like."

Their table by the window, outside of which stood Jocasta at attention, had candles on it, but the days were at their longest and daylight persisted. Moon, like Andy, Kate thought, was at his ease with women; not till later did Kate realize there had not been another man in the restaurant. He is older than Andy, Kate thought then, it is more original, more lovable in him.

After a time they pushed back their chairs and, for a miracle, did not talk of Harvard. "I'll sing you a song, Kate," Moon said, "to replace your smoke." And he played and sang songs new to Kate; she doubted if she would remember them, but it was a moment of communion, and she felt good. Outside the window, Jocasta too had given up all thought of food and lay down.

When it was dark, and goodbyes had been said and addresses exchanged, the two of them, Moon and Kate, walked back together, down Hampshire to Cambridge, Cambridge to Maple, down Maple to Broadway because Kate had a friend who lived on Maple Street, and it seemed a good idea to pass her house, and then down Broadway to Prescott, by Warren House to bid it farewell—"And hello," Moon said; he had never been inside the place all year—down Quincy to Mass Avenue, and along Mass Avenue to Harvard Square. "I've got my car down in the public parking lot," Moon said. "But I'll walk home with you before taking off."

"You don't mean you're leaving right now for Minneapolis, in the middle of the night?"

"That's the idea," Moon said. "If I get tired, I'll pull up somewhere and sleep."

"Wouldn't morning be a better time to start?" Kate asked.

"It would," Moon said.

"Sylvia's gone back to Washington. Why not start in the morning; at dawn, perhaps?"

"Why not?" Moon said, hoisting his guitar onto his shoulder again. So they walked along Mount Auburn Street together. When were they likely to meet again? Kate wondered. Harvard had marked Moon's last flirtation with the establishment. Was she ever likely to get to Minneapolis? She mentioned this to Moon. "Never mind," Moon said. "There's only now. There has always been only now, but it's at our age that you know it."

The 1979 Harvard Commencement Exercises were more bearable than Kate had dared to hope. For one thing, she was not asked to attend, as were Leighton's parents, the Garden Party, the Clambake, the Senior Class Picnic, the Masters' Reception or the Class Day exercises. She sat in her fine seat under the old trees in the Harvard Yard, and watched the graduating classes march in, and the faculty, and those receiving honorary degrees. The only speeches were by graduating students: one from the law school, a man and woman from the undergraduate colleges, the man's speech in Latin.

Listening to the speeches, Kate recalled an event she had read about that took place at the Commencement of 1969. A law student, addressing an assembly like this, here, she supposed, under the same trees, had begun his speech with a call to law and order: "The streets of our country are in turmoil. The universities are filled with students rebelling and rioting. Communists are seeking to destroy our country. Russia is threatening us with her might. And the republic is in danger. Yes, danger from within and without. We need law and order! Without law and order our nation cannot survive." After wild applause, the law student continued: "Those words were spoken in 1932 by Adolf Hitler." Kate would have given a great deal to have heard the silence that followed.

There was no silence now, only applause. Then the degrees were awarded. One woman received an honorary degree, a woman scientist unknown to Kate or, she gathered from the audience about her, to anyone else. She, and the young woman who had made the speech, and the president of Radcliffe, were the only women to set foot upon the stage. Dear Harvard, Kate thought.

In between there were songs or, as the program rather forthrightly put it: "To vary the somewhat monotonous bestowal of earned degrees, the Commencement Choir and the University Band at suitable intervals render music." Kate could not see Leighton, but would see her later at the smaller ceremony at South House. Sitting now under the trees, Kate felt benign and a little sentimental about Leighton; that she recognized both feelings as false did not prevent her enjoying them to the full. Kate's brother and his impossible wife, Leighton's parents, would, of course, be at the South House ceremony. But Kate had read her invitation carefully, and it said cocktails would be served. She looked forward to that.

Epilogue

Radcliffe is supposed to participate actively in the formation of policies affecting women and to serve as a strong advocate for women in a University community that has a history of sluggishness in providing education for women. . . . A woman's advocate faces a formidable workload at Harvard . . . where only 11 women hold tenure posts—less than 3 per cent of the number of full professors.
Harvard Crimson
Commencement Issue

SYLVIA FARNUM, Washington, D.C., to Kate Fansler, New York City:
. . . The great news, my dear, is that there is a new search committee for a woman professor of English at Harvard and I am on it. I believe there is even to be a companion female for me, Harvard having grown rather wary of lone females at their meetings. I need hardly tell you that this time we shall pick someone who can tell them what for instead of bursting into tears, and who may even be prepared to take on some of the problems of women at Harvard. A modernist, I rather think. Those in earlier periods seem to insist upon a simpler form of life which is not viable now, and I suspect was never very realistic. George, by the way, quite misses our Cambridge pied-à-terre and wonders if you and Reed would care to spend a vacation punting on the Charles. I saw no punts, but George says we were not looking at the right time. I understand that

Janet's university has set up a scholarship fund in her name. And how are things going back in . . .

Leighton Fansler to Kate Fansler:
Dear Aunt Kate, Father has more or less thrown me out, and I am living in a neat place on First Street and First Avenue otherwise known as the Lower East Side, and I have joined a splendid theater company. We are doing a production of *The Winter's Tale* and I'm going to play Pauline. Will you come to the opening night which . . .

Reed Amhearst to Kate Fansler:
. . . It's settled and I'm flying back in a week at the latest. Hope you have recovered from Harvard? I think I prefer the Third World to Harvard, except for the fact that you were there. It is called the Third World, I now know, because you were always with me in the other two.

Dean of Arts and Sciences to Professor Kate Fansler, Baldwin Hall:
Dear Professor Fansler: Welcome back from Harvard to your old home ground. We are, of course, all delighted to have you back at the old stand. On the recommendation of the University Committee on the Future of Education in the Faculty of Arts and Sciences, I am pleased to invite you to serve as a member of that body for a term effective immediately. . . .

About the Author

Amanda Cross is a pseudonym for a New York City university professor of English literature. She has written a total of six Kate Fansler mysteries: IN THE LAST ANALYSIS, THE JAMES JOYCE MURDER, POETIC JUSTICE, THE THEBAN MYSTERIES, THE QUESTION OF MAX, and DEATH IN A TENURED POSITION. Ms. Cross' first mystery, IN THE LAST ANALYSIS, received a scroll from the Mystery Writers of America for being one of the three best first novels of the year, and her newest book, DEATH IN A TENURED POSITION, received the 1981 Nero Wolfe Award for mystery fiction.